The
Daughters
Daring
& The Crystal Sea

Steven J. Thompson

STEVEN J. THOMPSON

Copyright © 2017 by Steven J Thompson

Illustrations Copyright © Steven J Thompson

Permissions Department,

KECELJ Publishing,

PO Box 577, Biggs, CA 95917

For information about the book and the author visit:
www.daughtersdaring.com

ISBN **978-0-9967232-2-0**

Illustrations by Steve Ferchaud

Cover Design by Cindy Grundsten

Printed in the United States of America

First U.S. Edition

Acknowledgements

If you are a returning reader of The Daughters Daring, let me begin by saying, "welcome back!" Much has happened from my first book up to now. My children, ever the source of my storytelling ideas, have started growing up. My oldest now serves in the United States Air Force, keeping us all safe and making her family very proud. Her younger sister keeps a busy life raising farm animals and participating on the high school track team. Their little brother continues to annoy them both.

There are so many I need to thank for helping me reach this point. My fellow members of the North State Writers Club in Northern California. They help with ideas and inspiration when I feel like quitting. My editor, Lynn Tosello, who keeps a tight ship on a sea of bad grammar. Even the best writers will always need editors, my friends. My artists, both for the cover (Cindy Grundsten) and interior art (Steve Ferchaud), who give life to my imagination. Alter Ego Costumes, again, for making my daughters look great on the cover.

Then there is my wife. She is the other person who sacrifices the most for my writing. She not only gives up her time to me while I peck away at my keyboard, but she is the lead designer who puts my words into a suitable publishing format. She is the quiet worker in the background who lets me bask in the glory, and to whom I am forever grateful.

Finally, I find that while my children are the inspiration for my stories, it is you, the dear reader, who give me the strength to keep writing. How much easier it would be curl up on the couch every evening after dinner and after a long day at work. How much simpler to lose oneself with the TV or even reading someone else's books. But you keep me going. After we had published the first book of The Daughters Daring series, I learned what it was to have true readers and fans. It's fun, but it's also a responsibility. I know you've been waiting for my next work, and I owe it to you to present my very best. I hope this story will not disappoint.

Table of Contents

STEVEN J. THOMPSON

Prologue

Emily, Interrupted

Emily Daring wiped her brow and took up a fighting stance: knees slightly bent, with feet a shoulder's width apart; a small wooden shield strapped to her left arm. Her sword in her right hand, raised above her head the way her father had shown her. She reminded herself to breathe as she and her opponent circled each other, watching for a moment of weakness in which to strike.

The morning sun was still fresh in the sky, lighting the rooftops and towers of Highcynder's capital city of Alcyndra, but not yet reaching into the courtyard behind Daring Manor. Over the city wall, the songs of morning birds could be heard within the enchanted forest where the first colors of fall were appearing. Beyond the manor, the sound of early morning workers could be heard in Alcyndra's market district. And if one caught the wind just right, the smell of Whipperpeel's baked goods could be detected.

Tobias Ocwen stood opposite Emily Daring. At 15, he was fully a year older than she, if only slightly more muscular. He brushed back his hair, reddish like his father's, and readied himself to attack. Like Emily's family, the Ocwens were Highcynder nobility, although not as highly stationed. Tobias was concerned that while it would be embarrassing to be bested by a younger girl, he also did not want to harm the daughter of Highcynder's most famed family. The fact that he found her annoyingly beautiful also confounded him. But he was a baron's son, and he would not show hesitation. He stepped in to make the first attack.

Whack! Tobias' sword clattered off Emily's shield as she deflected his blow. She returned with a jab at his waist, but he defended with his own shield. She had overextended, and he rammed her with his shoulder, pushing her to the ground.

Emily tucked and rolled, coming up with sword and shield in place to fend off Tobias' frontal assault. They parried and jabbed, back and forth, each looking for the advantage. Then Emily made a mistake. Feinting high, she hoped he would take the bait while she lunged in. Instead, he swung low, hitting her in the shoulder.

"OUCH!" Emily shouted.

"Oh dear!" Tobias said, taking a step closer and instantly regretting his victory. "I'm terribly sorry. Did I hit you too hard?"

"No, it's fine," she answered, rubbing her shoulder. "Just smarts a little."

"Please, let me," he said, leaning in to gently rub her shoulder.

He stood just a little taller than Emily, and she found herself looking up at him. For a second their eyes met, and she felt the strangest sensation as her heart started to flutter. Tobias' cheeks reddened like his hair as he realized he was staring into her blue eyes.

"Are you sure you're all right?" he asked.

"Uh huh," Emily said with a nod. She felt herself leaning closer to him, but she didn't know why.

"Look out!" A voice screamed from the window above.

Emily and Tobias looked up to see a bright blue ball of energy bounce out of the window and onto the roof ledge of Daring Manor. Behind it, Periwinkle, the garden gnome, was chasing after it with a small stick. The ball of energy seemed to laugh as it danced away from Periwinkle's clumsy attacks.

The two bounded off the roof and into the hedges before bursting back into the courtyard. Emily raised her shield in time to deflect the magic ball, which bounced down to Tobias' feet. Never fully stopping, the ball hovered momentarily just at his toes.

"I have you now, brigand!" Periwinkle shouted as he swung his stick, completely missing the ball and hitting Tobias in the shin.

This time it was Tobias who hollered in pain as he clutched his leg and hopped away from the gnome and the dancing ball. The ball bounced back toward Emily, but this time she was ready. Swinging her wooden sword with the flat side out, she smacked the ball clear across the courtyard, and right into her father's chest.

"What in the blazes is going on here?" Duke Daring demanded. The magic ball of energy bounded out of the courtyard and down the street. Periwinkle had slunk back into the hedges while the duke's eyes were on his daughter and Tobias.

"Father," Emily answered. "Tobias was just helping me with my sword technique."

The Duke stepped into the courtyard followed by Baron Ocwen. They had been in discussion inside the manor. Lately, the Duke had held a lot of private conversations with other nobles and members of the Knights

Council. Emily only knew that it was about the future of Highcynder and that it sometimes left her father rather irritable.

The Baron was a stout man with pale skin. He was fond of wearing fine cloth with beautiful embroideries that Emily thought were a bit much. Looking at him, she saw little resemblance between father and son, save for their red hair. As she found Tobias kind of handsome, she wondered if he got his looks from his mother.

"Emily, I heard you cry out," the Duke said.

"It was nothing," Emily answered, "we're just using wooden swords."

"I beg your forgiveness, my lord," Tobias said, taking a knee. "The fault was mine."

"Well," the Duke said, trying not to show his surprise at Tobias' respectful gesture, "this is rather unseemly."

"I'm sure my son meant no harm," the Baron said. "Come along Tobias. We really must be going now."

"Yes of course," the Duke answered. "I'll walk you out."

"Thank you, Duke Daring," the Baron said, "for your kindness and for meeting with me to discuss our kingdom's fate. These are trying times, and I appreciate your wisdom."

Emily heard the men talking as they walked out, but couldn't actually understand them. Her eyes and thoughts were clearly on Tobias Ocwen. When they were gone, she cast her glance back to the upstairs window, and Elizabeth. She glared at her younger sister.

"Oh, what now?" Elizabeth exclaimed.

"You know full well, Elizabeth!" Emily yelled. "You play innocent, but you always manage to ruin my life!"

"Emily Daring!" Duchess Daring reprimanded, as she stepped out of the manor. "What is the meaning of this?"

Emily threw up her hands and stormed off past her father who was just returning. Elizabeth smirked and closed her window behind Periwinkle as he scampered in, the magic ball of energy apparently forgotten.

"What was that all about?" the duke asked.

"Oh, just our daughters showing some of their less admirable qualities toward each other."

"And the Ocwen boy?" the duke asked. "I know I allowed for Emily to practice swordsmanship, but does she have to practice with a *boy*?"

"Darling," the duchess said taking his hand, "you can't keep her a child forever. She is growing up."

"But that boy…" he started.

"Is harmless." She finished his sentence.

"Is that what your mother said about me?" he asked, taking her in his arms.

"No. My parents knew you were a scoundrel from the beginning."

"Me?" he said incredulously. "I was the epitome of manners and class."

"You cavorted with a pirate dwarf, you scalawag!"

The Duke laughed heartily and kissed her. After his meeting with Baron Ocwen, he needed a good laugh.

"Just promise me you'll keep an eye on our daughter, and both eyes on that boy!" he said.

"I will," she answered, before looking at the upstairs window. "But she's not the daughter I'm most worried about."

STEVEN J. THOMPSON

Chapter 1

The Circus

Elizabeth Daring paced her room in near darkness. It had taken her weeks, perhaps months, to recreate the spell which brought life to raw energy. The witch had cast it with such ease, then tempted her with it. She could still remember the prickly sensation, the rush in her veins, as she felt it the first time.

Now she had successfully cast the spell but could not control it! The little ball seemed to have taken on a life of its own and then bounced out the window and was gone. Weeks of preparation and study gone; she would have to start over. She began to wonder if her obsession with the magical arts was a waste of time.

She had spent the better part of the last year reading whatever she could on the subject. To her dismay, most of what she had found pertained to parlor tricks and simple herbalism, which her mother insisted on her studying first. Finding anything to do with actual, real magic was next to impossible, and anything she found of substance took weeks of study to produce even the simplest of results.

Fortunately, she did have some reading of substance. She flipped through the pages of the novice spell book she found in the king's library. There were sections on how to channel magical energy, starting with exercises teaching mental discipline. After that came incantations; words that had to be perfectly pronounced while focusing the mind and directing the necessary elemental energy.

She had attempted numerous times to summon the electrosphere. It was, of course, based on the elemental school of lightning and required the use of a divining rod. Now she had finally succeeded, only to have it escape. How was she supposed to control it?

She continued turning pages, and there it was, just past the incantation. A footnote on the proper handling of the electrosphere. Elizabeth smacked her palm to her forehead and groaned. It had been there all along. Had she taken the time to read through the actual incantation she would have seen how to control it. Still, the witch had taken none of these measures and could summon one at will, effortlessly. For Elizabeth, the mere summoning had so physically drained her that she wouldn't be able to attempt it again until the next morning.

"It's hopeless!" she said, plopping down in the chair at her desk and slumping her shoulders.

"What's hopeless?" Periwinkle said from his perch on a shelf up above.

"How am I supposed to become a master of the magical arts," Elizabeth started, "when a mere incantation leaves me utterly exhausted?"

"Maybe you're just hungry," Periwinkle answered, rubbing the velvety doublet that barely contained his protruding stomach.

"It's more than that," she continued. "I have to cast more spells to get better, to gain more strength. But how can I do that when I can only cast one a day? No wonder so many wizards are old fogies!"

"I knew a wizard once," Periwinkle said as he stared at the ceiling. "Now, he was an old fella! His beard was so long that I hid in it once as some goblins attacked us. Of course, it turned out they weren't really goblins, they were just some forest gnomes. But by then I was tangled up in his beard. Boy was he ever angry!"

"You're not helping!" she said sternly. "There's got to be a way to speed up my learning! Perhaps a potion that could recharge my strength?"

Elizabeth searched through the book her mother had lent her, but the remedies and cures found there were slow and modest. At that moment it occurred to her that her mother likely hadn't shared all of her knowledge. There were plants in the deeper parts of her mother's garden that hadn't been described in any of the herbalist's guides Elizabeth was thus far allowed access to. Could her mother be keeping books with more potent recipes locked away somewhere? She resolved to find out when the opportunity came.

"Elizabeth?" her mother said, knocking on her door.

"Yes, Mother?"

"Are you all right?" Aryanna asked as she stepped into the dimly lit room. "Rather dark in here, isn't it"?

"I'm all right, Mother," Elizabeth answered. "I have a candle for reading."

"A candle? No illuminance spell?"

An illuminance spell, Elizabeth thought. *Why didn't I think of that?*

"No, Mother," she said, sighing, "I'm not yet skilled enough for something so *advanced*."

Aryanna noted the sarcasm in Elizabeth's voice, along with some defeat. She sat down on her daughter's bed, noting that the room was poorly kept.

"Liz, try not to be so hard on yourself. Magic takes years to master, and even then, it can be very dangerous if misused."

"I know," Liz said, hanging her head as she sat next to her mother, "but I've been working so hard."

"I know you have," her mother answered, "and that's what worries me. I agreed to let you study basic herbalism and healing remedies. Why do I get the feeling you're experimenting with more dangerous spells?"

"Mother," Elizabeth said, sitting upright now, her shoulders square, "just because you and the faeries drove the witch away, it doesn't mean she won't be back! I have to prepare myself!"

"That's not your job, Elizabeth!" Aryanna said, shocked at her daughter's defiance.

"Why?" Elizabeth said, standing up. Am I supposed to play swords with boys like my ridiculous sister? Or would you rather I waste my time in a garden, like you?"

"That's enough!" Aryanna shouted. "You are going to take a break from this and get outside again. Your father received word that the circus is arriving soon. You and your sister will be attending!"

"Mother, Emily and I helped save the kingdom from a witch with an army of goblins and ogres. Don't you think maybe I've outgrown the circus?"

"Be that as it may," Aryanna said, "you are still my daughter, and you are going to the circus."

"Very well," Elizabeth said, her shoulders slumping again. "I'll go."

"Good," Aryanna said. "And Elizabeth, please don't trouble your father with this newfound independence. He's already having a hard time with your sister growing up, I don't think he'll be able to handle it with you as well."

"But of course, Mother," Liz said sarcastically, "If it makes you happy I'll bow and curtsey as I ask him for money."

"Magnificent, dear," Aryanna answered back, trying to hold back a smile, "but your attendance will suffice."

As the sun started to set along Highcynder's western coast, a ship appeared on the horizon. Brig Baysong, Highcynder's dock master, thought it odd for a ship to be coming in so late in the day, but it wasn't the first time. There had been another strange ship just hours before. That particular ship carried an odd band of misfits: a dwarf, an elf, and a Dublarian girl among their crew. It just meant he would be working a bit later this night. It was his job to check in arriving boats and to find out their business.

For as long as he remembered, Highcynderians had remained mostly sheltered from the outside world. Everyone had heard stories of dwarves, elves, goblins or trolls, but few had ever actually seen them. The great ogre battle nearly two years before and the ensuing peace between the king and the gnomes seemed to have opened a floodgate. Now all races were arriving on Highcynder's golden shores, and he was pleased with his own acceptance.

Brig breathed in the ocean air mixed with the musty smell of his tiny wooden office. The last rays of the sun were shining in through the one window he kept clean to watch for incoming ships. Sunset on the Crystal Sea was a beautiful sight that even an old dockhand like him could appreciate.

Brig wasn't his real name. Brighson was the name his mother gave him, but he preferred "Brig." It was a nickname given him on the docks due to his thick, barrel-chested frame and rough hands. A brig was a mid-sized ship known for its thick hull and sturdy build. They were also his favorite ships, so the name seemed to fit. On his desk sat a small bronze replica of his favored sea vessel he'd been given years ago.

In his years on the docks, Brig had seen his share of merchants and emissaries. He'd escorted naval officers and tussled with a few of their sailors. He'd also seen his share of smugglers and pirates. He'd been around enough to know when a ship was bringing trouble, and the ship coming in, now, gave him that familiar feeling of foreboding. He waited until they were docked, then immediately boarded.

The first thing Brig noticed was the captain's food-stained shirt and shifty glances. His long coattails also gave him away as not having been a seafarer for very long. Experienced sailors kept their jackets short to avoid getting caught up in the lines. Sunburned skin completed the story, telling Brig this was not an experienced man of the sea.

"Dock Master on board!" Brig said in his bellowing voice. "State your business."

"Good evening, kind sir," the captain answered with a slight bow.

At least he has manners, Brig thought.

"Welcome to Highcynder," Brig replied, somewhat relaxed. "What is your business and cargo?"

"Ah yes, my cargo. I have some very special cargo all the way from Dublari."

"Nothing special ever comes from Dublari. Just swords and trinkets," Brig answered, stiffening his shoulders again. "If it's swords, you'll need to obtain permission from the Royal Guard."

"It is neither swords nor trinkets, my good sir!" The captain exclaimed with excitement. "What I carry on this ship will be in high demand by Highcynder's wealthiest nobles!"

"And that is?" Brig crossed his arms impatiently.

"Servants!" the captain answered. "A hold full of healthy, Gharidian servants purchased at a Dublari port just days ago!"

"Servants, or slaves?" Brig asked. Now he really didn't like the new captain.

"Ahem, well, slave is really a crude term, my friend." The captain answered, attempting to pass a small bag of coins to Brig, who kept his arms crossed.

"So first you call me crude, and then you try to bribe me." Brig scowled.

"My apologies, sir. I meant no offense," the captain stammered. "Here, I have a letter of invitation from one of my customers that you can look over."

Brig didn't like slave traders. It was a despicable occupation, although not exactly illegal. He would have preferred to turn them away, but not without first seeing the letter. The seal identified its author as Baron Ocwen. Brig sighed. A baron's signature held more weight than the suspicions of an old dockmaster.

"Very well," Brig said, handing the letter back, "you're cleared for now. Keep your crew and your cargo to your own vessel, or I'll boot you from my port. Understand?"

"Obviously, sir. Thank you!"

Brig turned away from the shifty captain and headed back to his office. It was already getting dark, and he needed to close up to leave when the night's watchmen came. He grimaced to see two more ominous individuals standing in front of his desk.

"Can I help you, gentlemen?"

The bigger of the two jumped a bit and put his hand on the hilt of a dagger tucked in his belt. On his back, a two-handed sword was strapped to his leather jerkin. As Brig's eyes adjusted, he could see that the big one was actually a half-orc. Full orcs were terribly uncivilized and didn't make office visits. His skin was dusky with a green hue, and two bottom tusks curled up over his lip. The other one, a human, was smaller in stature and wore dark robes with several pouches on his belt. Sandy blonde hair poked out from under his hood.

"My apologies, sir," the robed one said while grabbing the half orc's hand. "You startled my companion."

"I have that effect on some people," Brig said as he surveyed them carefully. If the slaver captain had seemed suspicious, these two struck him as downright dangerous.

"Now, who are you and what's your business here?" Brig demanded.

"My associate and I just arrived from Dublari and were hoping to find accommodations and, *information*?" The robed one revealed a coin purse as he talked and Brig grimaced at the second attempt to bribe him in one evening.

"The Salty Bard Tavern should have room for your type," Brig answered. "It's at the top of the road after you leave the docks. Can't miss it. Now if you two will excuse me, I need to be closing for the night."

"Yes of course," the robed one answered, pocketing the coin purse. "We'll leave you to your work. Thank you for your assistance."

Brig stepped aside from the doorway to let them pass, watching them carefully. The half-orc glared back at him. Brig noticed that the brute was slightly bigger than he was but didn't let it show. He wouldn't be intimidated in his own office. He watched them leave the docks and head up the hill toward town.

Brig thought for a moment about the newcomers before closing and locking his office. He hadn't seen either of them before and certainly didn't trust them. He realized that he hadn't caught their names and cursed himself. Then he noticed his bronze ship was missing and cursed some more.

"Wake up!" Joseph Daring ran up and down the halls of his home, yelling at the top of his lungs. "Wake up, wake up, wake up! WAAAAAAKE UUUUUUUP!!!"

Emily rolled over and groaned, still sore from yesterday's swordplay. She'd hoped to sleep a bit later, but her little brother was making enough noise to wake the whole house and at least five neighbors down the street. She could also hear her father laughing, a sign that he was responsible for Joseph's elated yelling.

Then her door burst open, and Joseph came spilling in. No longer a toddler, he had mastered door handles, but still hadn't learned the importance of respecting privacy. He was now more annoying than ever.

"Ugh, get out!" she groaned as she tried to crawl deeper into her blankets.

"Emily! Wake up!" Joseph insisted, as he ran forward and threw back the curtains. Light poured in making sleep even more futile.

"Joseph, what do you want?" she said, not hiding her irritation.

"The circus! Father says the circus is here!" He was jumping around as he spoke.

"The circus?" Her voice was muffled as she pulled the pillow over her head.

"Yes!" Joseph answered, ripping the pillow away. "Hurry, and Father will take us!"

"Yeah, Emily," Elizabeth said from the doorway, "aren't you anxious to go to the circus today?"

Elizabeth was already dressed in a simple woolen kirtle and a hooded mantle. Mother would likely disapprove and want them both to wear something more stately, but Emily knew her sister would resist. She herself enjoyed the fame and attention they had won when they saved the kingdom, but it was a bit much for her younger sister. It was odd for Liz to be so eager to go back outside.

"Oh, not you as well, Elizabeth!" Emily answered. "Since when did you start coming out in daylight again?"

"Since when did you sleep past dawn?" Elizabeth sneered.

"Come on Emily!" Joseph chimed in, "Wake up!"

"I'm rather sore from yesterday. Maybe you could go without me?"

"No!" Elizabeth shouted with some irritation, then relaxed and tried to smile. "I mean, I couldn't bear to go alone, sister. Won't you please come with me?"

If Elizabeth's early rise didn't rouse Emily's suspicions, her strange behavior certainly did. Her sister was up to something, and it wasn't just the circus. Emily decided she had better go along if only to find out what mischief Elizabeth was plotting.

"Very well," Emily said. "Now both of you get out while I dress!"

The market district of Alcyndra was quiet that day. There was still the occasional worker and shopper moving around, but for the most part, the Shining City was empty. Everyone was filtering into the field, south of the city, where several large tents could be seen. An arena had been built, and a race track ran along the edge of the enchanted forest, toward the putrid swale, and back again.

The arena sat in the center. It was a square stage surrounded by wooden bleachers. Banners bearing the crests of all the noble houses were posted, and the royal crest of the king adorned the stage. Vendors selling savories made their way through the already crowded area.

The Darings were applauded as they made their way into the seats reserved for nobles. The duke and duchess waved in response, Emily and Elizabeth curtsied nicely, and Joseph gave a dramatic bow. The Duke was pleased to see several members of the Knights Council in attendance. King Lamont, however, was noticeably absent.

Emily looked around and finally spotted Tobias Ocwen, oddly sitting apart from his parents, Baron and Baroness Ocwen. The Baron was at the edge of the bleachers, and a hooded figure stood next to him. When the figure moved, Emily was shocked to see a long, green snout instead of a human face. It was a gharidian!

Gharidians were reptilian creatures that stood upright like men but had the skin of a crocodile. Their long, skinny snouts were mostly used for catching fish. Mostly living in the swampy regions south of Highcynder, they were not hostile creatures but usually stayed in remote areas and were fearful of men. Strangely, this one was here among humans. The cloak barely hid its true nature.

Aryanna Daring noticed the gharidian as well, as had most of the audience by now. She turned to Baroness Ocwen who was seated near her.

"Lucinda, is that a gharidian with Baron Ocwen?" Aryanna asked.

"You haven't heard Duchess?" Lucinda said, all too happy to share the latest news. "A ship arrived last night with servants from Dublari. My husband was the first to buy one at the auction this morning!"

"Dublari servants?" Aryanna responded with disdain. "Don't you mean slaves?"

"Well, yes," The Baroness answered, somewhat embarrassed now, "but not the mistreated kind like in the East. It has really caught on in Newcynder, I hear."

Newcynder. Aryanna had heard this as well, but now it was hitting home. Rumor had it that the slave trade had been reignited with high demand from Newcynder. No one knew for sure what so many slaves were being used for, but she was certain it couldn't be good.

"Yes, I've heard the same thing," Aryanna answered.

"I'm sure the baron could arrange one for you if you'd like, Duchess."

"No, thank you, Lucinda," she responded. "That won't be necessary."

"Oh, look!" The Baroness shouted, "Something's finally happening!"

Everyone looked around as the sound of bugles blared over the audience. A crier dressed in a bright calico tunic ran up to the stage.

"Ladies and gentlemen! Nobles and commoners! People of Highcynder! Prepare yourself for a show like no other! The traveling circus of Bartemus Trollbane has arrived!"

A procession of wildly dressed people emerged from the tents and ascended to the stage while a small band of minstrels played festive music. Several on stage began juggling, tossing items back and forth to each other in increasingly precarious positions. The audience cheered them on and laughed as jesters rolled across the scene. Then the music stopped, and a drum roll began. The jugglers parted off the stage, leaving a lone, masked swordsman.

"And now, from across the Sea of Fire, rescued from the vast desert by Bartemus Trollbane himself, a warrior like no other, the master of Dublarian Steel, Blade Serendi!"

The audience cheered again as the warrior raised two curved swords in the air. Emily gasped and could not look away as the warrior was surrounded by four armored fighters, each with swords of their own. They paced in a circle around their prey who stood his ground, paying them little notice.

Finally, the first attacker moved in, swinging high at the Dublarian warrior, who easily ducked, swept the attacker's feet out from under him, then spun to deflect the sword of another. One by one, the attackers swung, chopped, and lunged in vain as the mysterious warrior danced around them in a marvelous display of swordsmanship and acrobatics.

When it was over, all four were on the ground at the warrior's feet, miraculously with no bleeding wounds at all. The warrior bowed to the cheers of the audience and removed his mask revealing not a "he" but a "she" who promptly took a bow. Emily gasped, wide eyed. Blade Serendi was a girl!

37

"And now, from the dwarven lands of the frigid north, our ringmaster and fearless leader, Bartemus Trollbane!"

The audience looked around in anticipation but saw no one. A second drum roll began as everyone went silent. And then...

BOOM!!! A cannon rang out from behind one of the circus tents. In the air, a small figure could be seen flying up into the sky. The crowd gasped in awe as the figure spread arms to reveal it was a little person! He shot higher and higher into the sky until he reached his apex, and started plummeting toward the earth. A woman in the audience screamed at the sight, and people began to talk in hushed whispers about what would happen next.

But before the small figure came too close to the ground, he threw out a large silken sheet above him. It was attached to him with multiple thin cords. Instantly the sheet picked up the wind and expanded, markedly slowing his dangerous descent. The figure sailed down onto the stage and landed with a small thud.

The audience roared with delight! Never had a feat such as this been seen in Highcynder before. Everyone laughed and cheered as the little man stood and wiped his forehead in mock concern with a "whew!"

Bartemus Trollbane was short and stocky like any other dwarf, although few in Highcynder had actually seen any other dwarves before him. Most dwarves stayed in their home region in the north, where the climate was much colder. He wore his black hair tied back in a short tail and let his sideburns grow down into mutton chops.

"Top o' the morning, good Highcynderians!" Bartemus announced in a surprisingly deep voice for one so small. He jumped up on a stool with his arms outstretched. "We've got much in store for ye! A circus-like none ye's ever seen! Watch death-defying acrobats! Try your luck against the incredible Blade Serendi! And if ye dare, enter the domain of Mordane, wizard of the dark arts!"

The audience responded with sounds of delight. Elizabeth is especially interested in the presence of the mage, although she suspected it would just be a master of parlor tricks with no real magic. Emily could think only about the sword maiden. The gentlemen in the audience were pleased to hear there would be a wagering tent in the back, as well.

"But, before you go," Bartemus continued, lowering his voice and approaching the crowd, "I am told that Highcynder's greatest heroes are present. Will the Daughters Daring please stand up?"

Emily and Elizabeth stood and took a bow for the crowd. Even Joseph stood up and waved.

"And who is this young lad?" Bartemus asked, approaching the most youthful Daring.

"I am Joseph Daring, protector of Highcynder!" Joseph proclaimed to the laughter of the audience.

"Is that so, laddie?" Bartemus asked him, with a wink to his sisters. "I'll bet the king pays you well for such protection then?"

"Well, not really," Joseph answered, shrugging his shoulders bashfully. He realized now that everyone was watching him.

"No?" Bartemus responded, "Then what is this?" He pulled a coin from behind Joseph's ear, and the audience burst out in laughter again. Joseph looked wide-eyed at the coin and searched his ears for more.

"Bartemus Trollbane!" Duke Daring stood, and announced, "On behalf of Highcynder I welcome you, and invite you to stay at Daring Manor for your visit!"

The crowd cheered again as Bartemus responded with a gracious bow.

"Let the circus begin!" Bartemus cried out.

That evening, a man with sandy blonde hair and dark robes made his way back to the Salty Bard Tavern from the circus, his coin purse a tad heftier than before. As he entered, he was thinking to himself that Highcynder was a splendid place for a thief to ply his trade. A stale smell, of spilled mead and something rotten, assailed his nostrils. The sight of the tavern keeper, with a large nose and wrinkled brow, was even less pleasant on his eyes.

"Hey, Mr. Black," the tavern keeper snarled, "your associate up there's been making some noise. I don't want my rooms busted up."

"Apologies, good sir," Jefferson Black answered, placing a coin on the bar. "I will make sure he is behaving appropriately."

The tavern keeper grunted as Jefferson headed up the narrow stairs into a dimly lit hallway. The faint light there revealed stained walls and a floor caked with grime. What did the noisemaking of a half-orc matter in such a place anyway?

He opened the door after three knocks. Startling a half-orc was never a wise thing, especially in their business. The room was a mess, with an odor more rotten than downstairs.

"Gordon!" Jefferson coughed and buried his nose in his arm. "What the blazes have you been doing in here?"

"Sorry," the half-orc answered, rubbing his belly. "It's stuffy in here."

"Indeed," Jefferson answered, wondering for a moment why he continued to travel with his brutish companion. As always, Gordon had only to flex his muscles as a reminder. Jefferson had been caring for Gordon since they were both young wards of Black's Orphanage in Westhaven, a central city across the sea. All orphans there were given the last name of Black, and little else. Jefferson and Gordon were about the only family either had ever truly known.

"A gift from our friend," Jefferson said, tossing Gordon a small sack of pastries. Gordon quickly devoured them.

Jefferson opened the window for some fresh air, then dropped his coin purse on the night stand. "It's been a profitable day at least," he said.

As he sat on his bed he noticed the small bronze ship on Gordon's bunk, "but it could have been better had you let me pawn that garish trinket you found."

"It's mine," Gordon said, pulling the ship close to him and trying to stuff it in his belt.

"I'm not going to take it from you, dear brother," Jefferson stated, "but we're not here to collect keepsakes."

Gordon gave him a blank stare.

"It will slow you down," Jefferson said with a sigh. "But never mind that, I have spotted our quarry whom we were contracted to find, Bartemus Trollbane and his traveling circus!"

"Time to fight?" Gordon asked his hand on his sword.

"Not yet," Jefferson answered, leaning closer even though there was no one to hear them. "I have also found Highcynder's so-called heroes, the Daughters Daring. Our employer will want more information before we take action."

"Duke Daring?" Gordon made a fist and swung at an imaginary foe. "I could take him."

"I'm sure you could," Jefferson said, pondering the battle. "Although he is said to have defeated an ogre. But no matter. The new queen did not send us to engage the Darings. We are here to eliminate the dwarf."

"And then we get paid?" Gordon asked.

"Yes," Jefferson said. "And then we'll get paid. Now, as it is finally dark outside, let's get you some fresh air."

Chapter 2

A Secret Journey

It was only the second day of the circus, and it was even more crowded than the day before. It was a hot day, and the added foot traffic was kicking up a cloud of dust that boxed in the heat. Still, Emily Daring was giddy to be there. She had come with her mother and Joseph. Elizabeth claimed to be ill, and the Duke was in a meeting with King Lamont. While Emily didn't relish having to keep an eye on her little brother, she knew he would tire soon, and she would be able to learn more about the mysterious sword maiden.

And then, of course, there was Tobias Ocwen. Emily had seen him arrive earlier with a couple of other young men of noble families. Their attempts at acting more mature kept giving way to horseplay and laughter. She hadn't thought he had noticed her until he made eye contact with her from across the arena and smiled, ever so briefly, before turning back to his mates. Emily had been floating ever since.

Despite her elation, Emily hadn't forgotten her main reason for being there. She had watched — while following Joseph this way and that — the sword maiden practicing her art on foolish challengers. For only a few coins, Highcynder's bravest were invited to try defeating her. They would have three rounds of swords (wooden swords, of course), with a point scored for a clean hit. None had beaten her yet, although Emily was sure her father could; if he wanted to.

"Lady Emily?" a voice inquired.

She looked around to see who could be addressing her. It was Tobias Ocwen.

Tobias looked dashing in red. Emily couldn't help noticing, usually when she saw him, he dressed more modestly. Today he was wearing a fine doublet, embroidered with his family's crest.

"Oh, Tobias," she stammered. "How are you?"

"I'm delighted to see you here," he said, gesturing toward the sword arena. "I would be honored if you would stay and watch me try my luck."

"Of course," she said, then cautioned, "but she is really quite good."

"True," he said, sticking out his chin, "but I have a few tricks of my own."

With a noticeable strut, Tobias confidently approached the ring and presented his coins. A circus hand ushered him in. Tobias was offered his choice of wooden swords, and Emily was pleased to see he didn't go with the largest one. Points were awarded for a hit, making the lighter sword a smarter choice. The sword maiden carried two wooden swords with curved blades, similar to her steel ones.

The bell rang. Tobias and the sword maiden squared off. He attacked first with a feint, a parry, and a direct jab, all of which she avoided. She came back with both swords thrust forward, followed by a spin to the left, finally swatting him across his backside. Tobias yelped in pain as the circus hand yelled, "Point!"

Emily called Tobias over before the next round could start. When he was near, she leaned in and whispered to him. "She has a pattern. Thrust, then spin to the left. You can counter with a roll in the same direction."

Tobias nodded and stifled a smile. The sword maiden seemed to pay him little attention anyway.

The bell rang again, and Tobias stepped forward. The sword maiden let him have the first attack as before, but he changed it enough to not give himself away. Again, she avoided his attacks, and again she countered with a thrust, followed by a spin to the left.

Emily watched in anticipation as Tobias countered with a roll, just as she had told him. When the sword maiden finished her turn, Tobias was now behind her! He swung his sword in a low arc and caught the back of her leg! Everyone watching, including the sword maiden, was shocked as the circus hand yelled, "Point!"

The audience cheered, Tobias was the first person of the day to score a point! Tobias threw his arms in the air, soaked in the admiration, and bowed. He was genuinely enjoying the moment. When he'd had enough, Emily waved him over.

"Lady Emily! Did you see me?" Tobias asked. He was jubilant.

"Yes," Emily answered. "But you'd better change tactics now. She won't make it so easy again."

"Nonsense!" Tobias proudly retorted. "I have her figured out, now. Watch as I finish this!"

Emily shook her head as Tobias practically danced back to the center of the ring. As the sword maiden approached, Emily noticed that she had changed her stance and the way she held her swords. When the bell rang, Tobias tried to repeat his previous success, but the sword maiden was way ahead of him. Her swords flashed as she spun the other direction, somersaulted over him, swept his legs from under him with a kick, and finally touched both her swords to his chest for the killing point.

The crowd cheered again at the astonishing feat, and then again for Tobias when he caught his breath and got to his feet. The sword maiden cast Emily a curious glance as she left the ring to take a break. Emily cast a sheepish grin back, before helping Tobias to his feet.

"Well, you certainly finished that!" she said sarcastically.

"I suppose I got ahead of myself," he said, his face reddened.

"It's all right," Emily said, offering him her arm. "You have won the honor of walking my mother and me home!"

"I thought you would *enjoy* going home," Elizabeth said.

"Not really," Periwinkle responded from deep within Elizabeth's closet. "The enchanted forest is beautiful and all, but sometimes it's not very hospitable to a simple garden gnome like me."

Elizabeth stood outside of her closet, hands on her hips. She didn't want to go alone, and Periwinkle could be handy to have along, in a pinch. If only he weren't so stubborn!

"Oh, come on, Periwinkle!" Elizabeth said, flustered. "This is an important mission, and I need you. Are you really going to let me go by myself?"

"Well, uh, that is to say." Periwinkle was starting to relent.

"I'll throw in scones," Elizabeth said, with a wink.

"Oh, all right! I'll go with you," he said, "for cookies."

"Fine, cookies it is," Elizabeth said. "Now hurry and get into my pack."

"Oh marvelous," Periwinkle said cheerfully as he climbed up. "I'm really not a fan of scones. They're sort of like a muffin that got sat on if you ask me. Although I do kind of fancy a good sweetberry scone, cookies are still my favorite. Say, what kind of cookies do you have?"

"Would you just get in the pack?" Elizabeth stood looking at him with arms crossed.

"Oh, very well," Periwinkle said, climbing in. "Say, isn't this the book I found for you in your mother's armoire?"

"Shhh!" Elizabeth shushed him, although there was no one else home. "Just be quiet about that. Let's go."

With Periwinkle and the book safely stashed in her pack, Elizabeth made her way to the pantry and grabbed some snacks. Then she went to the trophy room off the entry, where adventuring gear was now stored. She found her bow and Emily's sling-staff there, hanging on the wall alongside their father's sword. Guests to Daring Manor were always invited by the Duke to gaze upon the Daring weapons that saved the day from the Great Ogre Invasion.

Elizabeth reached for her bow, then thought better of it. A bow might seem too aggressive where she was going. Thus, Elizabeth decided that her sister's sling-staff would be the more diplomatic choice. After all, the faeries were their friends, and she was going to need their help.

Duke Daring sat in a high wooden backed chair, gazing out the window of the king's courtroom. It wasn't a very comfortable chair, but it afforded him the best view of the shining city from anywhere in the castle. From here he could see the site of the battle — not even two years past — of the Great Ogre Invasion. He twisted the end of his long mustache with his fingers and reminisced about his day of glory.

"Am I boring you, Sir Daring?" King Lamont asked. He had summoned the Duke to discuss important matters in private. Much of the conversation, thus far, had been about trade difficulties with Newcynder, and the Duke wasn't one for economics.

"No! Of course not, Your Highness," the Duke said, returning his attention to the king.

"I was merely looking back on our great victory."

"More like *your* great victory," the King corrected, "for you and your family."

"All in service to our King, Your Highness," the Duke said.

"Oh, poppycock!" Lamont answered. "You, Aryanna, and your children are dearly loved by Highcynder's people. They would rather you wore the crown than me!"

"I can assure you, Your Highness, I have no desire for your throne."

"But you have thought of it, haven't you?" Lamont asked. "Be honest, I have sent the guards away so we can speak freely."

"Your Highness," the Duke began.

"Stop calling me Your Highness!" Lamont interjected.

"My King?" the duke asked.

"Lamont," the king insisted.

"As you wish, Lamont," The Duke acquiesced. "Perhaps every man thinks of being king, but I look upon your duties, the throne, the people."

"And?" Lamont asked.

"And it appears to me as an elaborate trap from which a man can never be free," the Duke said, with a sigh.

"Haha!" the king bellowed. "Bravo, Sir Daring! It is no wonder the people love you so! There must be a dozen barons and lords on the Knights Council scheming for the throne with their visions of grandeur, but you, you are ever a man of the people!"

"I'm not one for ceremony, Your, er, Lamont," the Duke said.

"Indeed." Lamont coughed and changed the subject. "Sir Daring, these are troubled times. The Knights Council feels that I have grown old and weak and they seek to depose me. We are on the verge of a naval embargo, if not total war, with Newcynder. Worse, there are rumors that Newcynder has a new queen!"

"I am aware of this," the Duke answered. "Do you think it is she?"

"Don't say her name." Lamont winced. "It is still too painful."

King Lamont winced again and looked away, perhaps trying to hide his pain. He coughed for a moment, as Duke Daring watched with some concern, then cleared his throat and regained his composure. *A king must always present strength,* he thought to himself.

Lamont changed the subject, "What of your conversations with the nobles?"

"There are still some loyal to the throne," the Duke answered.

"But?" the king insisted. He knew from the duke's facial expression that there was more.

"But, I suspect some of them are up to no good." The duke's shoulders slumped.

"You have sources?" the king asked, frowning as he leaned forward in his chair.

"I'm not that accomplished as a spy," the Duke answered. "It's just my gut feeling."

The room lay silent while the king scratched his chin, thinking over the information before him. The Duke steepled his fingers quietly.

"What would you ask of me?" the Duke finally said.

"War is coming, Sir Daring," Lamont said, gravely. "I want you to command my army."

"Certainly there are others?" the Duke objected.

"None with the combination of your experience and loyalty. I need you to convince the Knights Council to set aside their squabbles until our kingdom is safe. I need you to serve as my general."

A general! The duke's mind was flooded with thoughts of the great battles he could command! Highcynder's enemies would flee in terror at the sight of General Daring, banner held high, as he rode across the field of battle on an enormous horse.

Then something caught his eye. Down on the street below, following the path through the market district leading toward Daring Manor, he saw Emily. She was walking with a boy. Not just any boy, but the Ocwen boy.

"Now," Lamont continued, "there will need to be a ceremony officially naming you as my general. I should probably wear my royal robes, as well.

For reasons he couldn't quite understand, the duke's heart started to pound, and without explanation to the king, he hurried toward the door.

"Ahem, Sir Daring, where are you going?"

"My apologies, Your Highness!" the duke said, as he ran out the door. "I have most pressing matters to attend to!"

And then he was gone.

"What in the world could be more important than being my general?" the king asked the empty room.

"I almost had her!" Tobias exclaimed as he thrust his mock sword into the air.

"You did better than anyone else who tried," Emily declared. She couldn't help feeling a strange giddiness when around him. It was easy to forget that her mother and Joseph followed only a short way back. Joseph teetered and leaned on his mother; a full day of the circus had him worn out. Were his father here, he likely would be on his shoulders.

Citizens of Highcynder passed this way and that. Most of them heading home from the circus as well. Some stopped at street side vendors before heading home. Whipperpeel's Sweet Shoppe even sported a small line. Happy customers came out with armfuls of baked treats.

Emily walked with her hands-free, as Tobias had instructed the Ocwens' new servant, Gerrass, to carry the basket of apples she had stopped for along the way. Though awkward, she had to admit it was rather nice not having to bring the apples home herself. She worried that Gerrass did not look happy, but Tobias assured her that the Ocwens would take care of him. Perhaps she would talk to Father about getting a servant. After all, the Darings were certainly more favored in the kingdom than the Ocwens.

"You're right," Tobias said, agreeing with her declaration. "I will compete in the Tournament of Swords in the spring, and I shall win!"

"Maybe," Emily challenged. "I have given thought to enter myself."

Tobias laughed — loudly.

"You find this funny?" Emily asked as she slowed and turned to look at him.

"You? You're serious?" His incredulity cooled at the intensity in her eyes.

"Yes. Why wouldn't I be?" Emily answered, stiffening her shoulders. "I have successfully faced greater dangers than wooden swords!"

"Of course, Lady Emily," he said, trying to reason with her. "But these are real opponents. Grown men! Not goblins. And you won't be able to use a sling staff!"

Tobias fired imaginary rocks from an invisible sling staff. Perhaps, Emily thought as she watched him, at imaginary goblins. She watched their shadows stretch ahead of them as they walked in the setting sun and pondered what to say to him next.

"I am learning to use a sword just fine, Tobias," Emily said. "By spring, I should even be able to best you."

"Best me?" Tobias chortled, nervous again. "Lady Emily, you are such a jester!"

"You seem very confident, Tobias," she said calmly. Her anger had turned into a plan.

"I am. Why?" Tobias asked, not certain he liked where this was going.

"Well then, perhaps you won't mind a wager?" she said.

"You really are serious?" he said, still surprised. "Very well. What is your wager?"

"If I win, I want you to escort me to the Spring Ball." Her chin lifted as her challenge was delivered.

"The, the ball?" Tobias stammered. This was something he hadn't contemplated before. Balls were for older people dressed in stuffy clothing! Why would she want to go to one of those?

"Yes. The ball," she answered confidently.

"All right then," he said. "And if, I mean when I win? What will be my prize?"

"Well," she said, stepping closer to him. "What do you want?"

Emily looked directly into his eyes, causing him to fluster. He pulled at his collar and glanced around nervously. She just kept looking at him with a grin. *Why was she doing that? Why did girls have to be so...so...confusing?*

"Your father!" Tobias exclaimed fearfully.

"What?" Emily replied in annoyance. "What do you want with him?"

"No!" Tobias answered, stepping back from her. "Your father is coming this way!"

Emily looked up the walk to see her father approaching from the market district. He was moving rather quickly with his eyes set on her and Tobias. She also noticed that he did not look particularly happy. He was almost caught up to them when the Duchess suddenly cried out.

"Oh!" Duchess Daring stumbled forward, seeming to have caught her foot on something.

"Aryanna!" The Duke turned to help his wife, suddenly forgetting Emily and Tobias. "Are you hurt? Whatever happened?"

"I'm fine. Really," Aryanna said, pulling the duke's attention away from Emily. "Something tripped me."

"Tripped you?" the Duke asked, looking around.

"Darling!" she exclaimed. "Do you think it was one of those mischievous gnomes?"

"Gnomes!" Joseph yelled with delight, instantly revived from fatigue. "I want to see the gnomes! Where?"

As Joseph and his father peeked behind a fence and in some nearby hedges for the mysterious gnomes, the duchess waved away Tobias, who made a hasty retreat in the other direction. Gerrass set down the basket of apples and quickly followed behind him as Emily watched them go. When the Duke finished searching for gnomes, he walked over to Emily and looked around for the boy, who wasn't there.

"Father!" Emily exclaimed, wrapping her arms around him. "I have great news!"

"And what news is that, my dear?" he asked, somewhat more cheered, but still suspicious.

"I'm going to enter the Tournament of Swords!"

When the Darings returned home, the manor was quiet. The Duke was carrying a sleeping Joseph up to his room, while the Duchess checked on Elizabeth. Emily set the apples in the pantry across the hallway from the trophy room. It occurred to her that something was amiss. She stepped into the trophy room and looked around. Everything seemed in place but...

Her sling-staff was gone!

The only logical explanation was that Elizabeth had it, as she was the only one left at home. But why? Emily stepped out into the courtyard expecting to find broken pottery or windows, but everything was in order there. Her mother's garden was quiet, as well. Where had she gone?

"Elizabeth!" she yelled.

"I'm right here," her sister answered from behind her. "Why are you shouting?"

Emily spun around to see Elizabeth coming out of the house.

"Elizabeth," Emily said, "where were you?"

"I've been inside," Elizabeth answered. "I didn't feel well. I fell asleep in Father's chair."

"Funny, I passed Father's chair and didn't see you," Emily said, with narrowed eyes.

"Well, it was dark," Elizabeth said. She stood with one hand on her hip and cocked her head at her sister.

"Why did you take my sling-staff?" Emily asked, annoyed now.

"Oh, there was a nasty crow poking about Mother's garden. I'm sorry, I should have put it back."

"There you are!" Aryanna said from behind Elizabeth. She put her hand to her daughter's forehead. "And still warm, too. You need more rest."

"Yes, of course, Mother," Elizabeth answered.

Emily watched her sister go upstairs to her room, then went back to check the trophy room. The sling-staff was there, hung on the wall. She inspected it carefully, but nothing seemed amiss, save for some fresh dirt on the bottom end.

"What are you up to now, Elizabeth?" Emily asked quietly to herself.

From across the road, a shadowy figure watched Emily Daring retire into the family manor for the night. It was dark now, but he kept his hood low across his brow to avoid recognition. Not that subterfuge was much in need. The good people of Highcynder were amazingly trusting — a weakness that Jefferson Black knew all too well how to exploit.

"Baked goods, sir?" A voice from behind Jefferson gave him a start.

"By the dark arts, woman!" he scolded. "Never startle me like that!"

"Oh heavens, lad. I am so sorry." Annie Whipperpeel answered sarcastically. "Care for some scones?"

"I'm not really fond of scones," he answered with a hand in the air. "They remind me of a muffin that's been sat on and hardened."

"Take the scones, Mr. Black," she said sternly, then added, with a sly gesture, "and hand over some coin lest we look suspicious. I'm sure you've made plenty at the circus."

"Very well," he scowled as they made the exchange. "What news do you have?"

"Why it's all in the bag, good sir!" She answered cheerily, her demeanor changing as she looked past his shoulder.

"What's in the bag?" A gruff voice asked from behind them.

They both turned to see a short, stout figure, standing just in the shadows. The figure was not much taller than a child, but thrice thick in the shoulders. He stepped into the light where they could see him.

"A dwarf!" Jefferson exclaimed.

"Bartemus Trollbane, if you will." He nodded ever so slightly but did not extend his hand.

"Ah, from the circus." Jefferson smiled and gave a slight bow.

"Would you like to buy some pastries, Mr. Trollbane?" Annie asked him.

"No thank you, dear lady," Bartemus answered, with a wink toward Jefferson. "I'm not partial to scones either, sat on or not."

"Well," Annie said, somewhat offended, "there's no accounting for taste."

"Indeed," Jefferson said.

"And what brings you two to Daring Manor?" Bartemus asked, stepping closer to them.

"The Darings?" Jefferson exclaimed. "I had no idea this was their home. I am merely a passer in the night."

"And I'm a peddler of scones," Annie chimed in, smiling.

"Mm-hmm," Bartemus responded with skepticism, "and next you'll tell me that faeries flutter around the Shining City at night?"

The three fell silent as Bartemus waited for a response. He was clearly suspicious of them and wanted to know more. Annie nervously cleared her throat, buying time. Jefferson cautiously moved his hand to the dagger on his belt, hoping darkness would keep his motion concealed.

"Bartemus!" The voice of Duke Daring boomed from the manor entrance. "I thought I heard you out there. Whoever are you talking to?"

"Good evening, Sir Duke!" Bartemus answered looking back over his shoulder to see that Annie and Jefferson were now gone.

"I would introduce you to my new friends, but it appears they've moved on."

"Well, come inside then," the Duke responded. "We've much to catch up on."

Bartemus gave a final look down the street and peered into the shadows. Then he shook his head and crossed the street toward Daring Manor. Perhaps he would investigate the suspicious ones in the morning.

STEVEN J. THOMPSON

Chapter 3

A Dwarf's Tale

"Duchess Daring, I daresay this is the sweetest sweetberry cider I have ever tasted!"

Bartemus Trollbane had joined the Darings in the common room of the manor where they were all enjoying some of Duchess Daring's sweetberry cider. Even Periwinkle had managed a taste from behind the bookshelf when no one was looking. The Daring coat of arms hung above the fireplace, reminding all their family heritage.

"Why thank you, Master Trollbane," the duchess replied. "And please, call me Aryanna. You've known me for years now."

"Aye, my lady," Bartemus answered. "'Tis true, I have. Though I haven't seen hide nor hair o' ye since the day you married this rapscallion!"

Aryanna laughed, as Bartemus leaned over and elbowed her husband in the side. The children joined in on the laughter despite having no idea what a "rapscallion" was. The Duke just made faces at them, feigning insult.

"Have you honestly known our mother that long?" Emily asked with a huge smile.

"Why yes, lass," Bartemus replied while leaning toward the children. "And I've known your father even longer! Set sail with him, I did. Into the icy north."

"The Troll Wars," the Duke said with a shudder.

"Trolls?" Joseph asked in delight.

"Indeed, young lad," Bartemus said. "Terrible and giant trolls, with rocky skin and a smell most foul."

"Tell us more!" Emily demanded.

"I don't think Joseph should hear…" Aryanna started to object.

"It's all right, Darling," the Duke answered. "They should all know the story."

"I will try not to scare the lad, my lady," Bartemus assured. "It was the start of winter, and I had sailed here to Highcynder from my icy homeland in the north. My people, the dwarves, had lived in solitude for many years, you see, with limited contact with the world of men."

The daughters leaned forward in their seats. Joseph was excited, too, but he was also sleepy and curled up against his mother.

"I and my companions had come in search of help," Bartemus continued. "Our land was under siege from a horde of trolls.

Your father gathered knights and soldiers to aid in our cause."

"Father," Joseph said, holding back a yawn, "you fought trolls?"

"Let him tell the story, Joseph," the Duke said, a finger to his lips.

"The journey back was rough," Bartemus said. "Storms pitched the Crystal Sea into a frothy mess, tossing our ship this way and that! After that, when we landed in the north, winter had started. I realized, then, that the men of Highcynder might not have been cut out for such a frigid climate. I feared we would lose our allies before we reached our foe."

"Did they make it?" Emily asked as Bartemus stopped to enjoy more cider.

"Aye," Bartemus replied. "We marched nearly seven days into the north. With icy winds growing fiercer as we went, and the creatures of the north snarling at our heels. Finally, we found our foe. The trolls had organized, in fashion, against our home, Mount Steelcynder. They had laid siege on the mountain, trapping my brethren inside. Against most enemies, we ordinarily would have waited them out. Dwarves can live for years underground you see. But not the trolls. Their very presence poisoned the land, killing trees and vegetation and replacing it with twisted, black vine. Most foul!"

"That's a strange effect," Elizabeth chimed in. She made a mental note to find more research on the subject in the king's library, when time permitted.

"Indeed it was," Bartemus replied. "We could not allow them to destroy our lands, but we did not have a sufficient army to drive them out. This is why we needed help from your father and his men. They rode into the battle, flanking the trolls and disrupting their siege. It gave courage to the dwarves who stormed out into the fight, as well."

"And the battle was won?" Emily asked.

"It was," Bartemus answered. "But not so easily. Many men and dwarves were lost. Your father and I continued the assault after the trolls retreated. We followed them for days until they had left our beloved land. This was when we were trapped in the fiercest of storms, and your father nearly froze!"

The Duke wrapped his arms around himself and shuddered. Joseph was now happily asleep on his mother's lap. Stories always seemed to have that effect on him.

"But you saved him," Elizabeth stated.

"Yes," Bartemus said. "We sought refuge in a deep cave. Had to bring the horses in with us for warmth. Your father was blue and shaking from the cold. Even the fire didn't seem to help. We dwarves are a bit stouter, though, so I gave him my blanket on top of his. I had to keep watch for trolls anyways and couldn't sleep. Your father made it, of course, but I lost a toe to frostbite that night."

"It was also in that war," the Duke added, "when Bartemus earned the name of Trollbane."

"Well on that note…" Aryanna said as she hefted Joseph into her arms, "I believe it's time for children to be off to bed."

"Not yet!" Emily exclaimed.

"One more story, Mother," Elizabeth said. "Please?"

"Very well," Aryanna answered, "but quickly this time."

The Duke got up for more cider, smiling to himself. He was happy to see his friend entertaining his children. As he reached for the cider pot, he nearly caught sight of Periwinkle, who slipped back into a cupboard. Emily saw it happen and stifled a gasp.

"Are you all right, my dear?" her father asked.

"Yes, I'm fine," she answered. Sometimes it seemed silly to her, why they should keep Periwinkle hidden. The gnomes were allies of Highcynder now. But her father wouldn't like the idea of a gnome living in their home, alliance or not.

"What do you wish to hear about, lass?" Bartemus asked Elizabeth, who was nearly leaning out of her chair.

"Tell me about your vessel!" Elizabeth replied.

"My ship, you mean?" Bartemus asked. "The *Chainbreaker*?"

"Yes." Elizabeth pressed him. "Where do you sail?"

"Well," Bartemus said, scratching his chin, "I have sailed all across the Crystal Sea and south to the Sea of Flame."

"And what of Mount Cynder, and the Starry Isles? Have you seen those?" Elizabeth asked.

"Mount Cynder is hard to miss, young lass!" Bartemus said with his arms outstretched.

"And what of the Isles? Did you make land there?"

"One does not simply make land in the Starry Isles, my dear," Bartemus answered. "The inhabitants of those islands are considered to be, inhospitable, shall we say."

"You've fought trolls before," Elizabeth pressed harder. "You even have a sword maiden. Why would you be afraid to go there?"

"Elizabeth!" Aryanna scolded. "I think Bartemus has answered enough questions for now."

"But Mother, he must know!" she exclaimed.

"Elizabeth, that is enough," her father commanded. "To bed. Both of you."

Elizabeth's eyes flared, but she stifled her anger and nodded assent, then kissed her parent's goodnight.

"My apologies, Master Trollbane," she said with a curtsy. "And thank you for the wondrous story."

Emily likewise kissed her parents and bid goodnight to their guest. She and her mother exchanged looks as she followed her younger sister up the stairs. Aryanna motioned toward Elizabeth with her eyes, giving Emily a subtle request: *Keep your eyes on your sister!*

Emily turned round, one last time, to ask a final question. "Master Trollbane?"

"Yes, dearie," Bartemus answered.

"Have you encountered pirates?" she asked, as her parents turned to look at her quizzically.

"Aye," he answered. "That I have."

"Are the stories true, then," she continued, "about Pirate Blacktoe? The notorious one?"

"Ah," Bartemus replied casting a glance at the Duke, "I'm afraid most of those stories are but a myth, lass."

"Oh," Emily said. "Thank you, sir. Goodnight."

An hour later all was quiet in Daring Manor, save for the Duke and his favored guest as they sat in his trophy room sharing stories not meant for younger ears. Aryanna had gone to bed for the night along with the children. The men would likely be up for hours, their laughter echoing up the hall.

"I can't believe you told them about your toe!" the Duke said, laughing. "Does it still pain you?"

"I hardly notice it," Bartemus answered. "But I still have the nickname back home."

"Blacktoe?" the duke asked. "Like the notorious pirate?"

"My good Duke Daring," Bartemus smiled. "Those days are behind me!"

"So you say. Does that mean you have returned home?"

"No," Bartemus sighed. "I have not been back in many years."

"But what about the love of your life? The dwarf named Freida, wasn't it? I thought you were going back for her?"

"No. I'm afraid that ship has sailed, lad." Bartemus hung his head low as sad memories returned to him.

"I'm sorry to hear it, my friend. But I envy your adventures, now."

"You could come with me!" Bartemus' eyes lit up again. "Set sail with me on a new adventure!"

"I could not," the Duke answered, this time his head hung low.

"Why not?" Bartemus asked. "Your children are older. The kingdom is safe, is it not?"

"The kingdom is *not* safe," the Duke answered, more seriously now. "Have you heard of the new queen?"

"Of Newcynder? I have. Her minions have a high demand for slaves from Dublari. The increased trade has a lot of money floating south. Attractive targets for piracy."

"Why all the slaves?" the Duke asked as he leaned back in his chair. "And why gharidians?"

"The slaves are used for the harvesting of sea crystals," Bartemus answered. "Very dangerous work, but gharidians are naturally amphibious. That's all I know."

"I appreciate your insights," the Duke said. "The king has asked me to serve as his general."

"General? Bravo!" Bartemus clapped his hand on his leg. "This is well deserved, my friend."

"Thank you. You're a good friend, Bartemus. The realm is in danger, though. I fear the new queen is plotting great evil and war."

"I will find out what I can for you," Bartemus said. "I am leaving tomorrow."

"Where are you headed?" the duke asked.

"South, along the western coast, toward Dublari," Bartemus said, with a grin. "Where all the money floats."

As the conversation between the duke and his friend continued, a small solitary figure stood in the shadows of the hallway. Elizabeth was determined to learn as much as she could about the dwarf and his strange crew. She felt something behind her and realized she wasn't alone. She turned to see Periwinkle and put a finger to her lips.

Periwinkle put his hands on his hips with a quiet "hmmph" and turned to see Emily, hiding farther down the hall, watching her sister. Emily also put her finger to her lips. Periwinkle decided that the behavior of human girls was much too strange for him. He left the hall to search the kitchen for a tasty snack, and then crawl into a nice dark hiding place for some well-needed slumber.

Across town at the Salty Bard, Jefferson was reuniting with Gordon, who was even more dismayed from staying locked up in the small room all day. Orcs were known for being tribal and nomadic. They didn't take well to staying in small buildings. Gordon was only half-orc, but Jefferson could tell he was getting restless.

"Relax, dear brother," Jefferson said calmly, trying not to cover his nose. "I have a feeling our quarry is leaving soon. We will be following after."

Jefferson rummaged through the bag from Annie Whipperpeel. Amid the scones was a small crystal, no bigger than the palm of his hand. He took the crystal out and gave the scones to Gordon, who quickly devoured them.

"You enjoy those?" Jefferson asked.

"Mmm hmm," Gordon smiled, flashing his bottom tusks, "taste like bumpets!"

"What in the world are bumpets?" Jefferson asked.

"Orc food," Gordon answered. "Old Orc woman sit on biscuits. Make bumpets."

"But you weren't raised by orcs!" Jefferson exclaimed. "How would you know that?"

Gordon just shrugged his shoulders as crumbs fell down his chest. Jefferson sent him away for fresh air. It was dark now, and Gordon was smart enough not to draw attention. Enough revelers were returning from the circus that one odd fellow would hardly be noticed. Despite the threat at her gates, Highcynder was still a trusting kingdom.

With the room empty, Jefferson placed the crystal on the table. He sprinkled dust around it from a pouch on his belt and chanted an incantation several times. The crystal started to glow, an eerie light emanating from it. In the center of the stone, a woman's face appeared and spoke to him.

"Hello Jefferson," she said.

"What is your bidding, My Queen?" he answered.

"Spare me the pleasantries," she said. "Have you dealt with the dwarf?"

"We have found him," he answered. "But it is not safe here. He is with the Darings."

The new queen shrieked, blurring the vision in the crystal. Jefferson thought he saw something in her place, a monster's face. But she quickly composed herself.

"Do you want us to deal with the Darings as well?"

"No!" she quickly replied. "The Darings are mine! I hired you to kill the dwarf. I will pay double if you bring me the Daughters Daring. Am I clear?"

"As you wish, My Queen."

"And Jefferson," she added. "I want the girls unharmed. Make sure you tell that simpleton creature you travel with, as well."

Jefferson hid his anger, relieved that Gordon was not there to hear.

"As you wish," he said again, turning over the crystal and ending communication.

Chapter 4

The Stowaways

Brig Baysong paced the docks. He had two ships leaving that day, and although the weather was calm now, the hovering blanket of clouds and hazy sun told him storm tides are on the way. If they were going to leave, it needed to be soon.

"Dockmaster Baysong!" The voice bellowed across the dock.

Brig turned to see a dwarf, accompanied by a dark-skinned girl, coming up the walk. He was relieved to see that they appeared to be in a hurry. The captain of the slave ship had seemed less concerned with the safety of his ship and more concerned with the comings and goings of everyone else!

"Master Trollbane!" Brig called out. "I trust our fair kingdom was hospitable?"

"It was indeed, Master Baysong," Bartemus answered. "My only regret is in my departure."

"Then you should endeavor to return sooner this time," Brig answered. "Your circus will be missed."

Bartemus cleared his throat and held a hand up to the air. Then he began to sing.

"Farewell and adieu to your fair Shining City,"

"Farewell and adieu to your city so grand."

"For I must now set sail, all the way to Dublari."

"To the city that rests upon Cynder's great sand."

"Well sung, friend!" Brig exclaimed and clapped. "I love a good sea chantey, but now you should hurry, for a storm most beautiful and fierce is headed our way."

Bartemus thanked the dock master and settled up his docking fees. The circus had made out well, and he even left a tip to make sure all of his equipment was loaded with care. The dock master assured him he had hired a good crew that even now was finishing the job. They could see several workers walking on and off the *Chainbreaker* from where they stood.

What they didn't see was a young girl, with staff in hand and a pack on her shoulder, sneaking from the docks onto the dwarf's ship. She had carefully timed herself so that she could make it across, between the dock workers' trips back and forth. Elizabeth's execution was almost perfect, unseen by every set of eyes, save one. Her sister's.

Emily looked up the docks toward Bartemus Trollbane, who was exchanging farewells with the dock master. She was confident she could hear him singing, but couldn't quite make it out. After Elizabeth had crossed the gangplank onto the ship, another dock worker appeared. He was counting crates of supplies before final loading in the hold below, and taking his time about it too! Emily watched impatiently, noting that it wouldn't be long before the other workers returned.

Finally, he went below deck. Emily looked both ways and saw that her path was clear, but not for long. All Bartemus Trollbane had to do was turn around, and she would likely be spotted. Her jaw clenched as she thought of her sister. What in the world was Elizabeth doing?

Emily bolted across the gangplank and onto the ship. Whatever her sister was up to would have to wait until she had found her and pulled her from the vessel, kicking and screaming if need be. Making it onto the deck, Emily looked around. She didn't have much knowledge of ships, save for a tour with her father when she was little. Emily was pretty confident the intricate door on the quarter deck led to the captain's quarters. There were doors on the front end of the ship as well, but she feared they might be crew's quarters. Finally, she found hatches leading down into the hold of the ship. That was where cargo was kept, and where Elizabeth most likely was hiding.

Emily quietly climbed down a ladder into the first level of the hold. It was musty and dark. She hadn't thought to bring a lantern, and a light would only give her position away. Beams of light shining from the hatch and from cracks in the ceiling did little to illuminate all the dark corners, but at least she could see where she was going!

"Elizabeth," she whispered. "Elizabeth! Are you down here?"

She heard footsteps approaching. They were too loud to be her sister.

"Is someone down here?" the dock worker called out. "Hullo?"

Emily froze. If she were discovered now, she would be thrown off the ship without her sister. The ship would leave with Elizabeth on it! She carefully sank back behind a stack of crates and tried to quiet her breathing.

The dock worker looked around, certain he had heard something. He had the strange feeling he was being watched. Then he heard tiny footsteps running somewhere behind him.

"Who's there?" he called out into the darkness.

The footsteps ran past him. He spun around but saw nothing, then he heard another noise behind him. He turned around again, but nothing. Then the hatch above opened and slammed shut.

"Enough of this!" the dock worker said to himself. "The dwarf can count his own crates, I'm getting off this cursed vessel!"

Emily shivered. The dock worker was gone, but what had scared him away? She decided she needed to find Elizabeth and get off the ship before finding out.

"Elizabeth? Emily? Where are you my darlings?" Aryanna called out. "Breakfast is getting cold."

Aryanna Daring had looked in her daughters' rooms and was calling down the hall. The morning sun shone through the windows of the manor, lighting everything before her. She worried, though, that their home seemed a little too quiet. She called out again as she descended into the dining room.

"Ugh, why all the shouting?" the Duke groaned, coming in from his study. He'd been up a bit too late with Bartemus the night before.

"Good morning to you, too, dear," Aryanna answered. "Will Bartemus be eating with us?"

"No," the Duke answered. "He was planning to leave early. They set sail today."

"Pity. I think Elizabeth was fond of his sailing stories," she said, then called out again, "Girls, come down for breakfast!"

"They can't hear you," Joseph said, wandering into the room.

"Joseph." Aryanna and the Duke now focused on their son. "Why can't they hear me?"

"Well," Joseph said nervously, "I'm not supposed to say."

"Not supposed to say what?" Aryanna asked coyly, letting her husband know with a look that she had it under control.

"That they left," Joseph answered. He immediately winced as he realized his mistake.

"And where did they go?" she asked, trying to stay calm.

"Um, I don't know," he said.

"And when did they leave?" she asked.

"Well, actually, Elizabeth left first," Joseph said. "She told me not to tell anyone. Then Emily went after her, and she told me not to tell anyone, either."

"They weren't together?" Aryanna asked, her alarm growing.

"No," he said. "Can I have something to eat now?" He was hoping to change the subject.

"Darling," Aryanna said, turning to her husband.

"I'll walk down to the market district," the Duke said. "I'm sure they haven't gone far."

"I need to check something," Aryanna said as she went upstairs.

The duke grumbled as he put on his boots and headed for the door. He noticed, along the way, that Emily's staff was not in its place. The memories of the ogre invasion came back to him, and he considered taking his sword but thought better of it. The girls were more likely into mischief than another adventure, and as long as Emily was chasing after her sister, he didn't have to worry about any boys chasing after her — especially the Ocwen boy.

The Duke opened the door to find Tobias Ocwen, flowers in hand, standing at the entry. Tobias' eyes widened, and he gulped, even as he offered a sheepish grin.

"You!" the Duke growled.

"Elizabeth, where are you?" Emily said into the darkness.

She had searched the first level below deck with no luck. Time was running out, and she knew she had to hurry before the ship left the port. She heard the creaking of steps ahead of her as if someone was walking down a flight of stairs.

Seeing an old lantern on the wall, Emily decided that finding her sister quickly was more important than remaining unseen. She lit the lamp and headed toward the back of the hold. A ladder led down to another — even darker level.

"Liz," she said. "Are you down there?"

More footsteps. Emily steeled herself and descended into the darkness. The lantern gave little light and cast shadows off the support beams. She came upon an open area with many cots and hammocks. Chains with wrist-sized manacles hung on the wall.

Beyond the cots, a small office stood open. The desk was covered with ledger books and a lit candle.

"Is someone in there?"

No one answered, but she heard little footsteps again. Emily gripped the handle on the lantern tightly and entered the office.

"Hello?" she said.

Something moved in the corner of the room, behind a stack of boxes. Fearing rats, Emily kicked the boxes, and the top one fell over behind the stack.

"Owww!" a small voice cried out.

Emily pulled the boxes back to find…

"Periwinkle! What are you doing here, and where is Elizabeth?"

"Oh dear," Periwinkle said, still rubbing his head. "I am terribly sorry, Emily Daring."

"Sorry for what?"

Behind her, the office door slammed shut. She heard a key turn in the lock.

"I'm sorry too, Em," Elizabeth said from the other side of the door. "I didn't mean to drag you into this. You should have stayed home."

"Drag me into what?" Emily demanded. "Elizabeth, what are you up to? Let me out of here, now!"

At that moment, the ship lurched, and Emily nearly lost her balance. The ship was leaving port!

"I'm sorry, Emily," Elizabeth said sternly. "You'll just have to go with me."

"There's no way you're coming with me!" the Duke bellowed.

"But I wish to help, sir," Tobias answered, "if the Daughters Daring have uncovered another mystery!"

"Enough!" the Duke commanded. "Sit."

Tobias Ocwen sat as he was told without any further protest. Duke Daring was relieved that at least the boy had the good manners to follow commands. Perhaps he could enlist him in the navy and send him away. Far away. He turned to see Aryanna coming down the stairs with a look of dismay.

"Duchess," he said. "What is it?"

"My book," she answered. "They have taken a book from my armoire. It is a book of great power."

"Magic?" he asked.

"Yes," she murmured. "Darling, they don't know what they possess. It's not safe."

"Why did they take this book," he asked, "and where?"

"I can answer that." a small voice said from above them. Numerous small lights floated into the room, and a diminutive figure appeared before them.

"Iris!" Aryanna exclaimed.

"Faeries?" the duke asked.

"Faeries?" Tobias shrieked.

"Faeries!" Joseph exclaimed in delight.

"Duchess," Iris said, "is there an echo in here?"

"Never mind that," Aryanna said. "What do you know?"

"I'm afraid your daughters may be in terrible danger."

Emily pleaded with her sister. "Elizabeth, please! There's still time to stop this. We just have to apologize to Captain Trollbane, and he will surely bring us back home."

"I'm not going home, Emily!" Elizabeth protested. "I finally found a way to enhance my power and this ship will take me right to it!"

"Your power? You're doing this for some magic spell?"

"Ugh, not a spell. An ingredient," Elizabeth said indignantly. "I don't expect you to understand."

"Liz, you can't do this! It's too dangerous, and, and Mother will be furious with you!"

"Mother?" Elizabeth said. "Mother had the answer all along, and she hid it from me!"

"Perhaps she knew you weren't ready!" Emily chided.

"You would see it that way," Elizabeth said. "All you care about is playing with swords and that silly boy. They're so proud of you. Everyone looks at me like something is wrong with me!"

"Because you've been acting strangely, Liz," Emily tried to reason as she pounded on the door. "You're locked away in your room all the time. You just need to come out and enjoy life. Find something you're passionate about."

"Magic is my passion!" Elizabeth screamed and turned away.

The boat lurched again. It was rocking back and forth more fiercely now, and it was starting to make Emily's stomach queasy. "Elizabeth, please let me out. I don't feel well."

Emily heard the key turn in the latch. The door opened to reveal Elizabeth standing firmly, looking at her. Emily knew that look. Her sister had no intention of giving in.

"You're getting motion sickness," Elizabeth said, handing her sister a small pouch. "You'll get used to it eventually, but this will help for now. Swallow a pinch of it."

"Thank you," Emily said, as she stepped out of the office. "What is this place?"

"It looks like they store people down here," Elizabeth said, pointing at the manacles "and, apparently, against their will."

"What do you mean?" Emily asked.

"I overheard Bartemus and Father talking about the slave trade," Elizabeth said. "Bartemus seemed very interested in the money involved."

"But, he's a friend of Father's!" Emily exclaimed. "How could he do this?"

"I don't know, Em, but we need to proceed carefully," Elizabeth answered. "He may be a pirate."

"A pirate?"

"Yes. I found an old black flag down here as well. And then there's Bartemus' nickname."

"Blacktoe," Emily said, as a shiver of realization came over her.

"Yes."

"He is a friend of Father's," Emily repeated. "I'm sure he will understand our mistake. I will go up there now and...and..."

And the room started to spin. Emily's vision blurred, and she suddenly felt very sleepy. She sat on a bench to gain her wits, but it only got worse. In seconds she was slumped over and asleep.

"I'm sorry again, Emily," Elizabeth said as she lifted Emily's feet onto the bench and propped up her head. "Those herbs I gave you do more than cure stomach aches. When you awake, we'll be miles from home, and perhaps then you'll listen to reason."

Chapter 5

A Rude Awakening

Bartemus Trollbane held the wheel of his ship, carefully steering amid the receding waves as the sun peeked out from the horizon. His crew worked the sails, occasionally breaking into song. The sword maiden kept watch from the crow's nest, above.

"See anything up there ma' dear?" he hollered.

"No sign!" she called down.

"And our quarry?" he asked.

"Nothing yet! I will find them!" she replied.

Bartemus looked over his shoulder for good measure. The slave ship had followed them out of Highcynder harbor, but they were separated by the storm. He had worked the wheel most of the night and steered them through the worst of it. Now he was tired, and his clothes were wet. He longed for his quarters.

"Come down for now!" he yelled to his lookout. "It will be another two days, at least, before we spot them!"

Bartemus looked out ahead of them. It would be at least another day before they could see land, but there was plenty to look at. The sunlight reflected off the Crystal Sea, creating a spectacular show of lights that never ceased to amaze him. He breathed in deeply of the ocean air and wondered why so many dwarves chose to live in mountain caves.

Bartemus stepped off the raised platform behind the ship's wheel that elevated him enough to see. Similar platforms were built around the deck of the ship specifically for him. He was not one to let stature get in the way of what he wanted.

"Bartemus," a soft voice said from behind him, "A word?"

"Eh," Bartemus said, turning around. "Gaeron! What is it, my friend?"

Gaeron was an elf who, like Bartemus, had left his people for life at sea. While dwarves were known for being loud and boisterous, elves were known for being mysterious and quiet. Preferring this air of mystery, he performed in Trollbane's circus under the name of Mordane.

"Before you retire for the day," Gaeron started, "I think perhaps you should inspect our cargo. We seem to have picked up some passengers."

"Passengers, eh?" Bartemus said, touching the dagger in his belt. "How many we talking, lad?"

"Two, and very young," Gaeron answered. "You won't be needing your sword."

"I'll be the judge of that!" Bartemus declared as he headed toward the hold.

Duke Daring paced the docks impatiently. The storm had passed, leaving the morning fresh. It was time to depart, and he was not known for his patience. Aryanna and Brig Baysong stood with him. Annie Whipperpeel was there, as well. She had seen how upset the Darings were on their way to the docks and insisted she could be of assistance. Of course, she brought pastries for their journey.

"What is taking so long?" the Duke asked.

"Captain Truxton is one of our navy's finest," Brig said. "I'm sure he'll have his crew together, soon."

"Thank you," the Duke said. "I still don't see why you insist on coming, though, old friend."

"I could not stand by with your family in need," Brig stated. "Besides, I've been watching this harbor for too many years, now. I want to go back out to sea!"

"General Daring?" the captain called from the ship. "We're ready when you are, sir!"

"General, is it?" Brig inquired, with raised eyebrows.

"Word travels fast," the Duke answered.

Brig loaded their gear onto the ship. He felt somewhat responsible for letting two children stow away on a ship under his watch and vowed to help in every way he could.

The Duke turned to Aryanna and embraced her. "Remember what I've told you about the council," he said. "They are as cunning as they are petty."

"I will be all right, darling," she answered, her head on his chest. "The king wouldn't have appointed me in your place if he didn't feel I could handle them. You just focus on finding our daughters, and bring them back home swiftly."

"I will find them, my love," he said. "I swear it."

He kissed her, and they shared a final embrace. Aryanna, determined to be strong, brushed away tears. She wanted to go with him, but the king hadn't allowed it. His condition for allowing Duke Daring to leave was her service on the Knights Council.

"There now, dearie," Annie said, putting an arm around Aryanna's shoulder. "There are none braver than your husband. I'm sure he will find your daughters."

"Captain Truxton?" the Duke said as he boarded the ship.

"Yes, General Daring, sir?"

"I trust you've been briefed on the importance, and danger, of our mission?"

"Yes sir," Truxton said. "My men know the risks. I've commissioned a private ship that will be less conspicuous. The *Nimble*

Sapphire also has some armaments should we run into trouble."

"Let's hope it doesn't come to that, Captain," the Duke said. "Now let's get this vessel moving."

Emily Daring felt a weight on her chest like two small feet pushing down on her. Then she felt tiny fingers grabbing hold of her eyelids.

"Hello?" Periwinkle said as he lifted her eyelids. "Are you sleeping?"

"Stop it," she groaned, and sat up, as Periwinkle jumped down. "Where am I?"

"You're on a ship," Periwinkle said. "A rather cold and dark ship, I might add. Not at all like the smorgasbord of the sea that Elizabeth promised me."

"Elizabeth?" Emily said, her memory coming back to her. "Where is she?"

"Over here," Elizabeth answered from the shadows. "How are you feeling?"

"I've been better," Emily said, rubbing her temples. "You drugged me!"

"Yes. Valerian root. I'm sorry."

"Sorry?" Emily replied indignantly. "Sorry? How could you do that to me?"

"You weren't very reasonable. I did what I had to."

"I'm not reasonable?" Emily was shouting now. "You've dragged us out to sea!"

"Actually, you walked on board. You're too heavy for me to lug."

"Ohh! You think you're funny now?" Emily said furiously, as she paced the floor. "That's it! I'm going up there, and I'm going to tell Bartemus to take us back to Highcynder this instant!"

"Well good luck with that," Elizabeth said. "Sure, he used to know our father, but now he's a pirate. Or worse, a slaver. Do you really think he'll be so accommodating to a couple of stowaway children?"

Emily paused. She hadn't thought of the possibility that the dwarf captain wouldn't want to help them. Could he really be that bad of a person, or was Elizabeth purposely trying to play on her fears?

"I don't care," Emily said. "I'm going up there to settle this right now!"

"Let me save you the trouble," a deep voice said from behind them.

The daughters turned to see Bartemus Trollbane, along with his sword maiden, on the ladder. He did not look happy.

"Captain Trollbane," Elizabeth said, with a slight curtsy.

"Don't start that with me, lass," Bartemus responded, jumping down. "I do not take kindly to stowaways on my ship."

"We're not, I mean," Emily, started, then gained her composure. "Captain, my sister and I are terribly sorry. We only wish to return home."

"And I suppose you expect me to return you?" Bartemus answered, gruffly. "I'll lose two days of sailing if I double back to Highcynder now. More if the storm hasn't let up!"

"Take us with you, then!" Elizabeth countered. "We won't be a burden."

"Elizabeth, no!" Emily stomped her foot.

"Listen to your sister," Bartemus said to Elizabeth. "Where I'm going is no place for children."

"We're hardly children," Elizabeth said, arms crossed. "Where else would you take us?"

"Clever lass," he replied, scratching his chin. "You're not leaving me much choice but to take you back."

"Father, no!" the sword maiden said from behind him. "You promised!"

Emily and Elizabeth both looked at the sword maiden. She was young, perhaps only a couple of years older than Emily, but had a fierce determination they admired. She stood with hands on her hips, just inches from the handles of her swords. Her Dublarian features were beautiful on her brown skin.

"Jolaia," Bartemus sighed. "It is too dangerous to take them with us."

"Then throw them overboard!" Jolaia answered, with a wave of her hand. "We have waited years for this opportunity!"

"Captain," Elizabeth cut in. "You do not have to turn around or throw us overboard. My sister and I can be of help in your journey."

"You've got spunk, lass," Bartemus said. "But no doubt by now your father is looking for you. Still, I can't turn around, or my own daughter might disown me."

"So, you'll take us with you?" Elizabeth pressed, as Emily threw her hands up, powerless to dissuade them.

"I will take you as far as Dublari, Daughters Daring," Bartemus said. "But the journey will not be without peril, nor is it free. You will work to earn passage here."

Jefferson Black was not happy. The sea was never his favorite environ, and the previous night's storm had left him feeling ill. At least here on the deck, he could get some fresh air. As the small slaver ship broke the waves, the spraying mist cooled his skin.

His brother Gordon was faring much better. The half-orc seemed to have no trouble with the ship's rocking. He was enjoying the fresh air as well and practicing with his sword. The crew made sure to give him a wide berth.

"Have you found them yet?" Jefferson called to the ship's captain, who was peering through a spyglass.

"Not since the storm, I'm afraid," the slaver captain answered. Jefferson was not so impressed with the captain's seamanship, but he was currently their only option.

"See that you do," Jefferson warned. "You will lose more than our fare if they should escape."

At the sound of his brother's menacing words, Gordon lowered his sword. He stepped closer to Jefferson and bared his tusks at the captain, who tried to maintain his composure and went back to looking through the spyglass.

"We are on the same course as they are, Mr. Black," the captain said. "It will only be a matter of time before we catch up to them."

Jefferson walked Gordon away to the other end of the deck. "Brother," Jefferson said, in a hushed tone. "When we find them, it is of utmost importance to the new queen that the girls be kept alive and unharmed."

"What about the dwarf?" Gordon asked gripping his sword.

"The dwarf we will dispose of, and collect our bounty."

STEVEN J. THOMPSON

Chapter 6

Ballroom Ablaze

Aryanna Daring was in the hall of the king's court, sitting in the same high-back chair her husband occupied just days before.

Like her husband, she was having a hard time keeping her thoughts on the conversation at hand. It had been several days since her daughters had gone missing, and she was greatly worried.

King Lamont sat across from her in a similar chair. A small table between them offered green tea and a variety of baked goods from Whipperpeel's Sweets Shoppe. Aryanna was still too upset to eat, but the tea helped immensely.

"Any word?" Lamont asked.

"None yet, Your Highness," she said, as she exhaled stiffly. "They have messenger birds should they find anything, but it could take some time."

"Be brave, Duchess," he said, using her title. He was in a serious mood today. "Highcynder needs its most respected family more than ever."

"I'm told Captain Truxton is one of your best."

Lamont broke into a short coughing fit. His face was red and puffy. "The finest I could spare," he said, still catching his breath. "He will find them."

There was a loud crash in the hallway, and a helmet rolled past the open door.

"Sorry!" the young voice of Joseph Daring called out. Aryanna could have left him with a governess, but chose to keep him close by.

"My apologies, Your Highness," she said.

"Oh nonsense," he replied. "Those old suits of armor have been collecting dust for years. Let the boy have his fun while we talk."

"Very well," she answered, somewhat worried. The castle had become rather unkempt, and Lamont's indifference troubled her. "Why did you call me here?"

"My dear cousin," he said, "I need you to save my kingdom."

Joseph wandered around the hall, looking at the empty suits of armor on display. His attempt to climb inside of one had caused it to go down like a shiny metal tree. He had thought that it might be fun to try and topple all of them at once, but that would make more noise and likely get him into trouble. His mother was taking a long time. It had only been a few minutes, but to him, it seemed like hours! Joseph felt a terrible wave of boredom creeping over him. He looked around for something fun to do.

That was when he saw the ball of energy. It was clearly the one from Elizabeth's room. It had bounced off down the street, and somehow had ended up here in the main hall of the king's castle!

The ball was mostly hidden. Perhaps it didn't want anyone to know it was there, Joseph thought. Or maybe it just didn't want any grownups to see it. They tended to get upset about fun things like balls of magic energy bouncing around the house. Joseph was not dismayed and decided right away it was his job to catch the pesky ball. He could give it back to his sister when she came home from her trip. That would certainly surprise her.

One of the king's servants walked down the hall, carrying some table linens. She didn't see the blue ball of light and barely seemed to notice Joseph, for that matter. As he watched her go, he saw that she had left the linen closet slightly open. He decided to take a look.

"Hmmm, I wonder what they have in here," he said.

There wasn't much in the closet other than linens, some candlesticks, and a brass serving tray with a domed lid. It looked just big enough to hold that quirky ball of energy.

Something bumped his leg.

"Hey!" he shouted, as the magic ball bounced past him.

Joseph grabbed the tray and lid and ran off down the hall after the ball of energy, which seemed to be waiting for him to give chase. It was toying with him.

"I'll get you!" he shouted.

And the chase was on.

Aryanna Daring glanced nervously at the hallway where Joseph could be heard yelling. King Lamont seemed not to notice and motioned for his servant to pour them some more tea.

"What do you mean, save the kingdom?" she asked. "From whom?"

"I think you know," he said. He looked at Aryanna squarely now. She could see in his eyes that this had been eating at him for some time.

"But we drove her away," Aryanna stated.

"Yes, and now she is in Newcynder," Lamont answered.

"The new queen?" Aryanna asked, her voice slightly quivering.

"I believe it is she," he answered.

"Then, she is behind the slave trade?" Aryanna said, working out the details in her mind.

Lamont motioned for her to be silent as the servant returned to check their tea. They sat in silence until she left, Lamont watching her until she was gone. Aryanna watched Lamont.

"It is corrupting even our people, Aryanna," he said. "She is at the heart of it."

"They were never happy," she said. "Even with their own kingdom."

"Did you think me weak," Lamont asked, "that I let them go?"

It had been years since the Newcynder revolt. What had once been a great effort at colonizing the world of Cynder, nearly turned to civil war. Rather than commit forces to that horror, Lamont had acquiesced.

"You prevented a war," she said. "That took courage."

"But she never saw it that way," he answered. "She called me a coward when she left."

"She was filled with anger," Aryanna said. "She kept it hidden when we were young, but eventually it came out."

"You knew her even better than I," Lamont said. "She betrayed us both."

Aryanna's mind drifted to her daughters. They were out there, somewhere, and alone. Worse, the Darings' greatest enemy was out there as well, and more powerful than ever. The thought of her children being in danger made her shiver, but her husband was doing all that he could. For now, the King needed her.

Suddenly, Lamont was coughing again. This time it was fiercer than before. His face went red, and he was clearly struggling for breath.

"Your Highness, you don't look well," Aryanna said.

"I'm all right," he replied. "I've just been under the weather the last few days."

"What can I do?" she asked.

"I believe she has spies here," he took a long breath before continuing, "in the kingdom and even within the Knights Council."

"The council?" Aryanna gasped. "I realize some of them do not support you, Your Highness, but treason?"

"Is it so surprising?" he asked, scowling. "Look how quickly they adorn themselves in power and privilege! That is what she will offer them."

"And what is my part in this?" she asked.

"I need you to go to the council," he said. "If it comes to war with Newcynder, I will need you there to argue my decision."

"War would be terrible. Is it necessary?"

"I sincerely hope it is not. I do not wish for one drop of Highcynder blood spilled over some territorial squabble. But, I will do what I must, to save our kingdom."

"I will be ready to help," Aryanna said, now rising to her feet. "Now, I really must see where Joseph has run off to."

Joseph had been following the energy ball through most of the castle. Through a hallway and around the corner. Through a kitchen and back again (of course, he did stop to sample some treats). He followed it up the stairs, out onto a balcony (that one definitely would have had his mother worried). Back into the castle and into the king's private chambers. Finally, onto the interior balcony overlooking a large ballroom.

There were lots of musical instruments up here, and Joseph was tempted to stop and inspect them all. It might even be fun to try playing some of them, as he was sure he would be quite good at it! Then he remembered his quarry, the magic ball of energy. It was sitting on a chair next to a funny shaped string instrument (Joseph thought perhaps it was a lute). It bounced up and down, now, but stayed in one place. This was his chance!

Joseph leaped through the air, brass serving tray and domed lid in hand, and made a scooping attempt at the magic ball, only to have it bounce just out of reach. His brass tray hit the chair on which the lute sat. Both chair and lute toppled over into another chair holding a shiny metal trumpet. The trumpet tumbled and fell over onto another trumpet, just next to it, and then the two instruments fell onto another instrument on a third chair.

While the musical instruments were crashing like polished dominoes, the energy ball danced, as if in delight, to all the loud noises. It seemed to be so delighted that it had forgotten Joseph! Joseph crouched low now, creeping up on the annoying little ball. As he crept closer, he noticed that the ball was near a large tapestry that hung down from the ceiling and over the balcony ledge. It was a little old but still beautiful, hand woven and embroidered with the symbols of their kingdom. But Joseph was more interested in its use than how it looked. If he could chase the ball into the tapestry, he would have it trapped!

Joseph bumped into and tipped over the next row of chairs holding instruments, causing yet another cacophony as woodwinds and string instruments toppled into each other. Loud crashes echoed into the hall below, and the magic ball again danced in delight! The last instrument fell just where the ball of energy sat watching, forcing it to move backward into the tapestry.

Joseph grabbed the tapestry just as a tuba was crashing onto a cymbal. He draped the curtain over the magic ball (which was still paying attention to all the noise) and scooped it under, catching it!

"Victory!" Joseph yelled.

That was when he noticed the smoke coming from the tapestry. The smoke then turned into fire, which quickly climbed up the fabric toward the ceiling.

"Uh oh, that's not good!" Joseph said, with wide eyes. "I'm going to get in trouble!"

Joseph tried putting out the fire with more of the hanging tapestries, but it only resulted in catching more of them ablaze. His situation was beginning to get worse as the fire snaked along the ceiling and was now blocking the only entrance to the balcony! His eyes were also starting to sting from the smoke. He had to get out of there.

Joseph felt something bump his leg. He looked down to see the ball of energy there. It motioned him toward a final, large tapestry that hung all the way down into the hall below. It was also not on fire.

"You're right!" Joseph exclaimed. "I'll climb down it!"

Joseph grabbed the tapestry on both sides and gave it a firm tug. It was attached to some drapery that adorned the front of the balcony area but felt sturdy enough to hold him. Trying not to look down, Joseph climbed over the balcony railing and wrapped himself around the tapestry as best he could. Then he started to climb down as the magic ball watched from above.

Joseph lowered himself carefully, his hands already tired from his tight grip on the tapestry. He was below the balcony now, but still high enough that a fall could hurt him. Suddenly, Joseph felt something jolt, and he began to swing. Looking up, he saw that the draperies on which the tapestry was fastened were starting to come loose! If they all broke at once, he would fall!

"What do I do now?" Joseph yelled out loud.

The magic ball of energy bounced up and down, getting his attention. He watched as it then bounced into another tapestry, causing it to swing back and forth. Joseph followed suit and began swinging the tapestry by kicking his legs out, while still lowering himself closer to safety. As the top of the tapestry finally came loose, Joseph was now in full motion swinging down onto a table below and sending plates and goblets scattering. Joseph looked around and breathed a sigh of relief.

He was safe!

"Joseph Daring," his mother's voice yelled as she entered the hall. "What in the name of Highcynder have you done this time?"

STEVEN J. THOMPSON

Chapter 7

Battle at Sea

Emily Daring took up a fighting stance and raised her sword, her legs shifting with the rocking of the Chainbreaker as it cut through the waves. The sun reflected on the waves of the Crystal Sea, reflecting a rainbow of light that shown over the ship's bow. Emily was careful not to look directly into the blinding light.

Jolaia Serendi stood opposite Emily, her own sword at the ready. She no longer donned the mask of the sword maiden, having no secrets on her father's ship. The mask only got in the way of her training.

Though the two hadn't spoken much, they had found the mock combat a way to pass the time. Jolaia had incredible skill, but Emily was a fast learner. While Emily was still mad at her sister for their predicament, she was actually starting to enjoy their journey. She let a slight smile cross her lips as she charged her opponent.

Their wooden swords thudded and clacked as they slashed, parried, and swung away at each other. The crew had taken to watching the two spar, wincing whenever Emily cried out in pain and silently cheering her successes against the fiercer Jolaia. Whoever won, it was a break from the monotony of their journey.

"You're getting better, Emily Daring," Jolaia said as she swept past her opponent. "I think it is helping that you let me cut your hair."

"Thanks! Hmmph!" Emily grunted as she spun, swung, and missed. Less than shoulder length now, her formerly long hair was not on her face, and it gave her a sense of freedom. "I still can't seem to hit you, though!"

The two faced off again and lowered their swords. They dipped out a cup of water from a barrel (Emily noted it wasn't the freshest tasting water) and stood at the bow overlooking the vast Crystal Sea. The mist from the breaking waves below felt fresh on Emily's skin. It had only been a few days, but she was getting used to life at sea.

"It's not as easy when you are in the match yourself," Jolaia said. "Instead of coaching another."

"What do you mean?" Emily asked.

"In Highcynder," Jolaia said, "you told that boy how to hit me."

"Oh, that," Emily said, as they shared some water. "He's just a friend."

"But you saw my weakness," Jolaia said. "You are a quick study."

"And you're a good teacher," Emily responded. "Where did you learn?"

"A traveling swordsman who owed my father," Jolaia said.

"Bartemus?" Emily said. "He's not your real father, though."

"No. Bartemus found me when I was very young, and raised me as his own. He's the only father I have ever known."

"What happened to your parents?" Emily asked.

"I would rather not discuss this, Emily Daring," Jolaia said. "Look, off the bow."

Emily stopped and looked out to sea, along with several of the crew. Massive crystals jutted out of the water like spiny islands of glass. As the sun's light refracted through them, a rainbow appeared to emit in every direction.

"It's amazing," Emily said.

"Yes. This is a rare formation that has grown above water. Most are deep beneath the waves, but some are just beneath the surface. It can be as dangerous for ships as it is for those who are enslaved." Jolaia explained.

"They make them dive for the crystal?" Emily asked.

"Yes. This is why the slavers started using gharidians, instead of humans. The gharidians are amphibious creatures and are one of the few races who can survive the task," Jolaia answered. "But even for them, it can be perilous."

Emily tried to ponder the harshness of life for the gharidians against the beauty of the Crystal Sea. Only days before, she had looked at the Ocwen's servant with fancy. Now she was beginning to wonder if she was wrong.

"And that is why you help them?" she asked.

"That is why we help them." Jolaia nodded.

Whoosh! Emily and Jolaia ducked as a fireball shot out to sea, mere feet above their heads.

"Sorry about that!" Elizabeth called out. "Terribly sorry. Really, I am!"

Emily and Jolaia both cast angry stares at the younger Daring. While Emily practiced in swords, Elizabeth had been working just as hard in the magic arts. Gaeron, the ship's mysterious elf mage, had agreed to tutor her. Certain that their mother would disapprove, Emily had, of course, objected. But Gaeron suggested it would be safer for her to learn under his tutelage than on her own.

"At least this time you didn't catch the sails on fire!" Emily yelled out. "Mother would still not approve!"

"No more than she would approve of you cutting off your hair," Elizabeth retorted, "but I won't tell if you don't!"

Emily turned and stormed off, stopping only to look back at Jolaia.

"Be glad you don't have any siblings!" Emily said, in anger.

"Why would I be glad for that, Emily Daring?" Jolaia responded, "your sister brings you so much, *entertainment*."

Emily shook her head and continued to her quarters. The crew dispersed back to their duties, but they kept a careful eye on Elizabeth. Even with Gaeron's aid, she had still managed to catch the mainsail on fire.

"I'm beginning to wonder, lass," Bartemus said as he approached Elizabeth, "if you and your sister are more entertainment or trouble."

"Captain," Elizabeth said with a curtsy, "I assure you it's all in fun. I'm glad to have your attention, though. Are we any closer to the Starry Isles?"

While Bartemus had been enigmatic about their destination, Elizabeth decided now was a good time to seek answers. Mother's book had provided an idea of where to find what she was after, but it gave little details of what else would be waiting for them.

"Not that I am taking you there," Bartemus reminded her. "But why would you want to visit the Starry Isles anyways, lass?"

"There is a rare flower there that I need to collect," Elizabeth said.

"That's it?" he asked. "A rare flower? What does it do?"

"It enhances magic."

"Ah, I see," he said. "You're a novice mage, wanting to boost your abilities."

"Actually, yes," she responded.

"And why do you seek such power?"

Elizabeth paused before answering, looking away as she carefully chose her words. She then looked him square in the eyes and stood with her hands on her hips. "My kingdom and my family are in danger, Captain Trollbane. Wouldn't you do everything possible to protect those you love?"

"Ha!" Bartemus laughed out loud. "You have your mother's eyes and your father's stubborn determination! Have you considered the Starry Isles might be too dangerous for a young adventurer like you?"

"I have faced danger before," Elizabeth answered unwaveringly.

"Spoken like your father," Bartemus said, scratching his beard. "And it almost cost him his life."

"The Troll War?" she asked.

"The same. We were both lucky to survive that "little fracas." Your father didn't know when to quit, either."

"But you saved him," Elizabeth said.

"Aye, lass," Bartemus said, reminiscing. "And I don't fancy having to save you. The Starry Isles are a dangerous place. Better I leave you in Dublari, where your father can find you."

"But why the rush to get to Dublari if you can't stay?" Elizabeth asked. "What exactly is your mission, Captain?"

"Gods, lassie," Bartemus exclaimed. "Have your mother's wit as well, do ye? My mission shall remain secret."

"Captain!" A voice yelled down from the crow's nest. "A vessel off the starboard bow!"

Bartemus picked up his looking glass and ran to a platform on the deck that allowed him to stand taller. Jolaia was by his side in an instant.

"Is it them?" she asked frantically.

"Aye, lass," he said. "'Tis our quarry, indeed."

"Sail ho!" the yeoman of the *Desolation* yelled out.

The captain drew his spyglass and scanned behind them. It was a smaller ship than his, but it made up for size with increased speed. He frowned as the other ship rolled cannons into place, and raised a black flag.

"All hands on deck!" the captain yelled. "To your battle stations!"

The deck erupted in excitement and confusion. The crew was experienced enough to know what needed to be done, but their thus-far quiet journey had lulled the crew into complacency. They had been caught off guard, and they knew it.

"Is it him?" a crewman whispered. "Is it Pirate Blacktoe?"

"Quiet fool!" another silenced him. "You'll have the whole crew panicked!"

"Are we fighting, Captain?" the first mate asked him.

"We've no choice at this point," the captain responded. "They're too fast for us to out-run them. We'll see how they like some cannon fire!"

"And if they overtake us?" the first mate asked.

"Then we'll surrender. We have little cargo Blacktoe would want, I'm sure," the captain answered. "And no gold. We spent it on the slaves. Unless…"

"Not the sharpest swords on the sea, eh Captain?" the first mate said.

"That," the captain thought to himself, "or they have another agenda! Get me a carrier pigeon at once!" he ordered. "Then get me four crew members. I have a surprise in store for our pursuers."

"Aye, Captain!" the first mate answered, as he ran to his duties.

"The new queen will want word of this," the captain muttered to himself.

"Fire!" Bartemus called out the order for the first strike, hoping the other ship would surrender quickly.

The cannons roared as though thunder itself had landed on the deck of the *Chainbreaker*. Emily and Elizabeth covered their ears, but the sound was still deafening. The black smoke of the cannons clouded the air before blowing away in the misty wind.

The daughters had taken cover in the doorway of the captain's quarters. Gaeron had placed a protective spell over the ship and crew, but Bartemus wanted extra insurance for his royal passengers. Even the best of magical spells could not stop a full volley from the other ship's cannons.

Bartemus surveyed the slave ship. His first attack had disabled their forward sail and possibly two of their cannons. The enemy ship was both larger and slower, making it harder to line their sights on the *Chainbreaker* as well. A few more attacks and they would be completely disabled. However, the downside to being the smaller ship was that, the larger ship could carry more armaments. A mistake on Bartemus' part could mean disaster.

The enemy ship's cannons roared in answer.

"Incoming!" the crew yelled as they ducked for cover. Emily shielded her sister as best she could.

If the cannon fire had been like thunder, the impact of cannon balls on the deck was like the striking of lightning! Splinters of wood blasted through the air and sections of the main sail were torn through. Miraculously, no one was hurt beyond some cuts and scrapes from the blasts.

Bartemus grimaced at the damage to his sail. He needed the wind to provide his maneuverability in battle. He needed to land at least two more attacks on the enemy vessel before he had any chance of them surrendering.

"Tighten those sails and bring us about!" Bartemus bellowed. "Prepare to fire!"

As the crew scrambled, they paid little notice to Elizabeth Daring, who had left her shelter for a better look at the enemy ship.

"Elizabeth, get back here!" Emily demanded.

"They're not in a position to fire!" Elizabeth protested. "And I need a better look."

"A look at what?" Emily asked, now beside her sister.

"There! On the front deck!" Elizabeth pointed. "Those aren't cannons the crew is loading."

"What are they?" Emily asked.

"Captain!" Elizabeth screamed as loud as she could. "They have mortars!"

"Egads, you're right!" Bartemus answered as he looked through his spyglass. "Evasive maneuvers! Hard to port!"

The *Chainbreaker* reversed course just as the mortars erupted on the *Desolation*. Within seconds' fire rained down from the sky. Most of the rounds went into the sea, but a couple exploded over the deck. Gaeron's magic spell took most of the impact.

"Haha! That was close!" Bartemus yelled. "Bring us about! We'll position directly behind them and buy some time! Gaeron, if I take us closer, can you disable them?"

"All of my energy is devoted to our protection, Captain," Gaeron answered as he wiped sweat from his brow. "I cannot shield our ship and launch an attack. But perhaps the girl."

Their eyes turned to Elizabeth.

"Me?" Elizabeth asked. "But I'm not that powerful! Gaeron only taught me the fireball spell two days ago!"

"Here," Gaeron said, handing her a small vial. "Take this. It will enhance your ability temporarily."

"Is this?" Elizabeth stammered, her eyes fixated on the potion.

"It is," Gaeron answered. "Now drink it, quickly, and concentrate. You will be more powerful, but it will be dangerous to harness such energy."

"Dangerous?" Emily interrupted. "You can't endanger my sister like that!"

"Emily, it's all right," Elizabeth said calmly, putting her hand on Emily's shoulder. "I can do this."

"You'd best do something quick, lass," Bartemus shouted. "They're preparing for another shot at us!"

The *Desolation* loomed toward them as it slowly turned. Its sails were damaged, but it was still an ominous sight. Her crew could be seen loading the mortars even as others stood ready at their cannons. Any moment they would again fire upon the *Chainbreaker.*

Elizabeth quickly took the vial and drank it. She was surprised it didn't taste as bad as she'd expected, and it tingled as it went down. Within seconds she felt a surge of energy welling up within her, like a burst of adrenaline mixed with a great elation that she could not hold on to. She longed to release it.

"Wait," Gaeron said to her. "They're almost in position."

Bartemus turned the *Chainbreaker* again, swinging his ship around broadside. It would bring them in the range of the *Desolation's* cannons, but it would also give Elizabeth the opening to fire her spell. He would have to pray that the mortars would not yet be ready to fire.

"Stay down, Miss Daring!" Bartemus hollered. "But be ready to fire after the next attack. You'll only get one shot at this!"

The *Chainbreaker* caught up with and was broadside with the *Desolation*. Bartemus ordered his crew to fire first, but the *Desolation* was barely a second behind. Gaeron strained as the magical shield was pummeled, and random projectiles still tore through the deck. Gaeron went down on one knee.

"I am drained," Gaeron said solemnly while looking at Elizabeth.

Before the smoke could dissipate, Elizabeth was on her feet. The *Desolation*'s crew had taken cover but was back in place on the mortars. Knowing it would take some time to reload the cannons, they were adjusting their aim for firing. They wanted to hit the smaller ship with maximum effect.

Elizabeth felt the pressure of the magical energy within her. It felt as if it would seep from her pores if she didn't release it soon. In her mind, she summoned the words that would call upon the fireball spell and positioned her hands to control the direction of the blast.

"Now, Miss Daring!" Bartemus yelled.

Elizabeth barely heard the words escape her lips. It was almost a whisper compared to the roar of magic and fire that formed just in front of her. It grew between her hands until it was too large for her to contain. She could feel the heat, and yet it did not burn. This fire was hers. She focused again on the mortars, so close now she could make out the crew's faces. They were lighting their fuses.

Elizabeth let go of the fireball, which was now as big around as her father's shield. It hurled across the open space between the two ships and struck the mortar directly in the middle of the group. The mortar exploded in place, causing a chain reaction that exploded each of the mortars, destroying the entire front mast and two more cannons in the process.

Moments passed as they watched for retaliation. Then, a white flag waved from the *Desolation*.

"Huzzah!" Bartemus yelled as the crew cheered.

Elizabeth sank back onto the deck as Emily helped her. She felt drained of all energy as if she had just run three times around the walls of Highcynder. At the same time, she felt elated at the size of the spell she had cast.

"Are you all right?" Emily asked her.

"Yes, I'm all right," Elizabeth answered. "Did you see it? It was unlike anything I've ever done before!"

"It was… amazing," Emily said, a little concerned.

"Daughters Daring," Bartemus said, gesturing to his quarters. "If you would be so kind as to wait this out in my office?"

"Yes, sir," Emily answered, as she helped her sister to her feet.

"And the rest of you," Bartemus ordered, "Prepare to board!"

Emily and Elizabeth went into the captain's quarters as asked. They had done their part, and Emily feared to put Elizabeth, already dazed, at further risk. Bartemus' crew was equipped to handle it from here, anyway.

As they approached the captain's desk, they saw quite a mess. A platter that had once contained grapes, cheese and pastries was now mostly empty save for stems and crumbs. Next to the platter lay a sleeping Periwinkle, content with his hands on a full belly and crumbs on his shirt. Emily cleared her throat, and he awoke.

"Oh, um, hello," Periwinkle said. "Did I miss anything?"

Chapter 8
The Knights Council

Aryanna Daring looked around the room of the Knights Council. Grand tapestries and banners hung from the walls, along with swords, shields, and coats of arms. Numerous men of nobility were there as well, many accompanied by squires. Some even had gharidian servants. Aryanna was dismayed to see that, but for Annie Whipperpeel who was serving treats, she was the only woman in attendance.

"Lords," Duke Archibald announced, "and Duchess Daring. Will you please find your seats?"

The tables were formed in a horseshoe with the highest of nobility in the center. Duke Archibald sat at the head table. He gestured for Aryanna to sit next to him where her husband would usually be seated. Another chair next to her was left empty except for a boosting block commonly used for children.

"Duchess, is this seat taken?" A small voice asked her. Aryanna turned to see...

"Randolph!" she exclaimed. "You have no idea how happy I am to see you here. Yes, please, it seems this seat was saved for you."

"Thank you, Duchess," Randolph answered as he climbed into the seat. His chair had been boosted to allow the gnome leader to adequately address the council.

"I had no idea you were a part of this council," Aryanna said.

"As gnome ambassador, I have been invited to attend. Although they prefer I do not speak, which is rather annoying if I do say so myself. They are missing out on the story of how the gnomes came to help Highcynder in its time of need when the ogres attacked. Have I told you this story yet, Duchess?"

"If we may begin?" Duke Archibald called out, and the room quieted down. "We have gathered to discuss the matter of Newcynder's naval encroachments on Highcynderian waters."

"Duke Archibald," Baron Ocwen called out. "If I may be so bold, Newcynder is hardly an enemy. We are enjoying prosperous trade with their fleets, and I ask that the word 'encroachments' be stricken from the record."

"Very well," Duke Archibald answered. A scribe taking notes at a desk in the corner made the correction.

The room broke into conversation as various lords offered their input. It seemed to Aryanna that each was more interested in making their own statement than hearing what anyone else had to say. The conversation drifted back and forth between statements of Newcynder being their ally, to all-out declarations of war. There was also the question of why King Lamont was not more visible of late.

Aryanna carefully took mental note of who held which position. The room seemed divided, and she needed to know her allies. Baron Ocwen appeared to have the favor of several at the table who wanted more open trade with Newcynder. Sir Wormington, who had been knighted by Duke Daring himself, after the great ogre invasion, argued for increased security and caution. To his credit, Duke Archibald remained above the fray.

"I would hear from Duchess Daring," Archibald said. "Regarding King Lamont. I believe you have spoken with him?"

"Yes, I have," Aryanna said. "Our king fears the worst. That Newcynder's intentions, along with this new slave trade, are not for the betterment of Highcynder, and that Newcynder's new queen is certainly no friend of Highcynder."

"Nonsense!" Baron Ocwen blurted out. "Why does King Lamont not speak to this council himself, rather than let us hear from a woman who consorts with gnomes?"

The council gasped at Ocwen's words. Hushed whispers were drowned by outright shouting. Duke Archibald struggled to maintain control. Aryanna took a confused Randolph by the hand to lead him out of the room. She curtsied to Duke Archibald.

"My apologies, Duke Archibald," she said. "I will come back when they are ready to listen to reason."

"I fear that day will not come soon enough, my lady," Archibald answered quietly.

"Will we be there soon?" an agitated Duke Daring asked.

"Soon indeed, General Daring," Captain Truxton answered. "We are nearing the Dublari coast. We'll spot them."

"Not soon enough," the Duke said.

Duke Daring grumbled and watched from the bow of the *Nimble Sapphire*. They had been at sea nearly a week with no signs. Although Brig Baysong had reminded him it would be a long journey, his impatience was inflamed by his worries for his daughters.

"Don't mind him, Captain," Brig said. "He misses his children."

"As do I, Master Baysong," Captain Truxton answered. "These are not safe waters to traverse without an armada."

"And our disguise?" Brig asked, gesturing to the fishing nets and equipment strewn along the deck.

"It should work," Truxton said, "if we encounter Newcynder's navy or slavers. If it's Dublarian bandits, we may have to fight."

"Captain!" a crew member yelled. "Wreckage to starboard!"

They rushed to the rail to peer into the water as various bits of wood and flotsam drifted past. Smoke billowed up as some of the floating wreckage still burned. Duke Daring felt fear growing inside of him as he worried what had become of his daughters.

"Find their flag!" Truxton commanded.

"Here, Captain!" the crewman yelled, as he fished out the tattered piece of cloth.

"Who was it?" Duke Daring asked.

"It wasn't our friend the dwarf," Truxton answered. "It was more likely a slave ship. They bore the Newcynder colors."

"Who would sink a slave ship?" Brig asked.

"Captain!" another crewman yelled. "Sails to the north and south of us!"

"Blast!" Truxton said, peering through his spyglass. "They are Newcynder naval vessels."

The two ships were closing in on them quickly. Even from a distance, activity could be seen on the decks as they prepared their cannons and sails.

"It's a trap!" Brig exclaimed. "They'll blame us for the sunken ship!"

"Captain, we cannot be delayed," the Duke said. "Can we outrun them?"

"I don't know, General Daring," Truxton said, "but we'll certainly try."

"Land ho!" a crewman shouted from the crow's nest.

Emily and Elizabeth ran to the ship's bow for a look. They had been at sea for what seemed like ages now, and they were both eager to get back to dry land. They watched as the tiny coastline ahead of them slowly grew into an enormous port city.

"Is that it?" Emily asked. "Is that Dublari?"

"Aye, lass," Bartemus answered. "Southern jewel of the Crystal Sea and eastern gateway to the Great Desert."

"I've read about it," Elizabeth said, "but this is so much more…chaotic."

As the city drew closer into view, the daughters looked on in awe. The city seemed to stretch along the coastline as far as their eyes could see! In the center, an assortment of great, exotic buildings looked like palaces. Beautiful, with spiraling towers that twisted up into the sky, their tops adorned with large crystals.

As the city stretched out in either direction, the buildings were smaller and more dilapidated. Tiny shacks and hovels were packed around, and even on top of, each other, without any sense of direction or uniformity. Small pillars of smoke could be seen here and there, littering the sky above the city.

As disjointed as the city was, the port was much the same. Large, well-kept docks stretched out to sea from the city's opulent center, providing a home to enormous ships of all size and styles. But as the port reached away from the middle, the docks became more rustic. Tiny dinghies and fishing boats haphazardly bobbed on the water.

"It's not at all like Highcynder," Emily said.

"No," Bartemus responded. "Dublari is wild, like an untamed stallion. Dangerous like one, too. You must stay close to me, and heed my commands at all times. Understood?"

"Yes, Captain!" The daughters said in unison.

"And it doesn't hurt to bring your weapons!" Jolaia said with a wicked smile, as she tied her twin swords at her waist.

Bartemus steered the ship up the coastline aways, putting some distance between them and the opulent center. Soon, he found a decrepit looking dock with only one run-down boat that was covered in barnacles and decay. An unpleasant smell of dead fish and something worse drifted up to them. An old man fishing off the dock stood up and waved them in.

"Why are we docking here?" Emily asked. "It seemed much nicer, and safer by the palaces."

"Looks can be deceiving, lass," Bartemus answered. "This will be less conspicuous for us, in any case."

"If it's so dangerous," Elizabeth asked, "why are you leaving us here? Wouldn't we be safer on board the *Chainbreaker*?"

Bartemus paused and took a deep breath. He looked to Jolaia for support, but she only returned a quizzical look of her own as she stood next to the girls. His arms relaxed at his sides as he exhaled.

"Aye, it is dangerous," he answered. "But no more than at sea with me. I am harboring former slaves on board my ship, and someone will be wanting them back. I have friends here who can help with both the slaves' predicament and your own."

"And if that doesn't work," Elizabeth said, "you will take us on the rest of your journey?"

"You'll know soon enough," Bartemus answered.

As Bartemus and Jolaia left the *Chainbreaker*, another ship quietly docked at a safe distance. Jefferson and Gordon Black donned their cloaks and disembarked for Dublari's inner city. Jefferson had left instructions with the slave captain to stay put and out of sight.

"Where we going?" Gordon asked in a hushed tone.

"The dwarf has connections here," Jefferson replied. "People he would trust with both his business and with his cargo."

The Brothers Black passed through a small market. Stalls of every description lined the street with merchants selling assorted foods and wares. It was a hot day, and the crowds of people left Jefferson feeling suffocated and irritable. Gordon, however, seemed pleased with this setting and slipped a small figurine into his pocket as the merchant looked away.

"How we find them?" Gordon asked.

"We have connections of our own, dear brother," Jefferson replied. "We just have to find their connection first."

"And then?" Gordon said as they stepped into a narrow alley.

"And then you can put your sword arm to use," Jefferson said, holding his nose from the smell of the alley. "Hopefully, we won't be staying long."

Emily and Elizabeth followed Bartemus and Jolaia through the crowded streets. Throngs of people were scattered everywhere — merchants, workers, and beggars filled every space, making the enormous city look somehow smaller. Everywhere there were people and a multitude of sights. It was difficult for the girls to keep up with so much to look at. Several times they would have been separated, had they not been holding hands with each other and Jolaia.

"Try to keep up," Jolaia scolded as she looked back.

They were given a break as Bartemus stopped to allow a caravan to pass. A procession of wagons carrying gharidians passed them by. The gharidians were chained to the floors of the wagons and to each other. They were covered in dust, and several had lash marks on their backs. Guards with whips and swords rode on every wagon as well.

"We should help them!" Emily said, making a fist.

"Quiet!" Jolaia told her. "We are greatly outnumbered here, and your words will bring trouble."

Emily restrained herself and kept her cloak over her head as the caravan passed. They watched the slaves a moment before Bartemus led them to a narrow alley.

"My friend is here," Bartemus whispered, motioning to a small door. "I will go and explain our situation."

"Father, look," Jolaia motioned to the door. The handle had been bashed in.

"What the…" Bartemus started to say.

A scream from behind the door interrupted him. Jolaia went for her swords, but Bartemus put his hand on her arm. He motioned them back out of the alley and onto the street.

"What was that?" Elizabeth whispered.

"It wasn't good," Bartemus answered. "Let's return to the ship. I will come back and investigate."

"So we're not staying?" Gaeron asked.

"What do you mean we're not staying?" Emily Daring asked with tightly crossed arms. "We were supposed to wait here for our father!"

Emily and Elizabeth were in the captain's cabin with Bartemus, Jolaia, and Gaeron. On their return, Bartemus had quickly ushered them into his office. He gave orders to set sail immediately for the Starry Isles, and then returned to his favorite chair to catch his breath. The day's last sunlight reached through the windows giving its last life to the day's heat. Periwinkle could be heard lightly snoring in the corner.

"I am sorry, Emily," Bartemus answered. "But plans changed. It is unsafe for you, or any of us, in Dublari now."

"What happened?" Gaeron asked.

"Someone knew we were coming," Bartemus said, "and got to our contact first. They killed him."

Emily gasped. The others remained silent.

"So, we are going home?" Elizabeth asked, her eyebrows slightly raised with hope.

"Not just yet," Bartemus said solemnly. "The dock master here told me the Newcynder Navy is now patrolling these waters. We were lucky to have slipped in so easily. We must now leave under cover of night, or risk being caught."

"And you let the slavers go!" Jolaia scolded. "They will bring the Navy back for us!"

"We do not sink helpless ships, Jolaia," Bartemus replied, "any more than we would abandon the slaves we rescued. I am sorry we did not find your parents, but we will keep searching."

"I don't understand," Emily stated.

"The Dublari slave trade did not always deal in gharidians," Gaeron said. "Humans were taken as well."

"Jolaia's parents?" Emily whispered.

"They were supposed to be on that ship," Bartemus said. "Jolaia, I am sorry."

"So what happens to the slaves you rescued?" Elizabeth asked. "The gharidians."

"There is a place within the Starry Isles," Bartemus said. "At the base of Mount Cynder, there are ancient ruins where a city once stood. It could be a new home for them."

"Mount Cynder is where I need to go, as well," Elizabeth said.

"It is not safe there," Gaeron looked at her with concern.

"What do you mean it's not safe?" Emily asked.

"The ruins are said to be inhabited by evil creatures," Bartemus said. "But it's mostly legends. The rest of the island should be safe, but no one has really been there for some time."

"Except us," Jolaia said.

"But only on the shore," Bartemus added.

"Burying treasure, Captain?" Elizabeth asked, smiling.

"A pirate never tells, lass," Bartemus said with a wink.

"Wait," Emily said. "Why not sail home? We will be safe in Highcynder!"

"Newcynder's Navy will be patrolling the open waters," Bartemus answered. "With our damaged sails, we'd be nearly helpless. We need to hide, and bide our time."

"We can bide our time while we search the ruins," Elizabeth said. "It's perfect."

"No, it's not, Liz!" Emily cut in. "Our family is out there looking for us, and all you care about is your stupid flower!"

"And you just want to go back for that silly Ocwen boy," Elizabeth retorted, then mimicked her sister. "Oh Tobias, won't you take me to the Spring Ball?"

"Shut up, Liz!" Emily said, blushing. "How did you know?"

"What, really?" Elizabeth said. "I was just guessing. Besides, now that you've cut your hair like a boy he really won't want to go to the ball with you anyways."

Emily's face turned a darker red, and her fist closed tightly. Jolaia thought that Emily looked like a tea kettle ready to burst. This amused her.

"Ladies Daring, that is enough!" Bartemus stepped in. "It is a full night's journey to the Starry Isles. I suggest we all get some rest now. There is no telling what danger we may encounter there, and I will need all of you to help secure the island."

Emily and Elizabeth retired to the crew's quarters. They shared a tiny cabin with Jolaia, which gave them some privacy to change and sleep. Emily threw herself back onto her hammock and closed her eyes. She tried to imagine her parents and her home. She thought of Tobias, as well, and realized that she would probably not be home in time for the Tournament of Swords.

"You sure know how to ruin everything, don't you Elizabeth?"

"Oh please," Elizabeth replied from her own hammock. "You haven't exactly been helpful to me, either."

"What?" Emily said accusingly. "You're the one who got us into this mess!"

"No. I got myself into this mess. You didn't have to come along," Elizabeth said indignantly.

"I'm your sister! Of course, I followed you!" Emily said.

"Oh? Why?" Elizabeth demanded.

"Because sisters help each other."

"Good. Then you won't mind helping me find what I'm looking for on Mount Cynder? I could use your help."

"Fine then! I'll help," Emily said. "You are such a brat sometimes."

"Yes, I know," Elizabeth answered. "And I'm sorry for what I said about your hair. I think it suits you."

"Nice to hear you are in agreement," Jolaia cut in, also from her hammock. "May I please have some quiet now? We need our rest."

"Yes, Jolaia," Elizabeth apologized.

"Jolaia," Emily said. "I'm sorry we didn't find your parents."

"I am sorry, as well, Emily Daring," Jolaia said. "But I will not give up."

"We won't either, Jolaia," Elizabeth said, looking to her sister who nodded back. "We will help you find them."

"Thank you, Daughters Daring," Jolaia answered. "Now good night."

"Good night."

Chapter 9

Treachery, Discovered

"Incoming!" someone yelled.

Duke Daring and Brig Baysong took cover on the deck and tried not to get in the way of the crew. It was chaotic, but somehow the *Nimble Sapphire* hadn't been hit yet.

"A miss!" another crewman yelled as cannon shot could be heard hitting the water behind them.

"Truxton knows his craft!" Brig said, leaning into the Duke. "Either that or he's incredibly lucky."

"Let's hope he's both," the Duke answered back. "See if you can get a look at the ships. We may learn something for later."

"Aye," Brig said as he brought his own spyglass to his eye.

There were two ships that Brig could see circling them, both flying the Newcynder flag. Whenever they tried to position broadside for a shot, Captain Truxton would skirt ahead of them. Truxton's ship was smaller and faster in close quarters. On the open sea, though, the larger ships would overtake them, forcing them into a dangerous game that Brig feared wouldn't last end well.

Then he saw the third ship.

"Blast!" Brig said, pounding his fists on the ship's railing.

"What is it?" the Duke asked.

"We're going to need a bigger boat," Brig said solemnly.

The Duke grabbed Brig's spyglass and peered out to sea. An enormous warship was closing in from the north. He couldn't make out much more, but it also flew Newcynder colors. He put down the spyglass and ran to the ship's wheel.

"Truxton!" the Duke yelled. "You've seen them?"

"Yes," he answered. "It's a class one warship — slow, but carrying superior firepower. We've no chance of beating them."

"And outrunning them?" the duke asked.

"I've managed to get us closer to a string of small islands along the Dublari coastline," Truxton said. "If we can stay out of reach we can outmaneuver them. They won't be able to follow us in the shallows without the coral reef tearing their hull open and sinking them."

Duke and Brig looked out over the bow. Sure enough, they could see a group of small islands with a narrow pass through them. The pass looked barely wide enough for their own ship, let alone the naval vessels.

"It just might…" Brig started, but then his voice trailed off.

"Might what?" the duke asked. "Brig, what is wrong?"

Brig had gone silent. He was staring off into the distance as if entranced. Then the Duke realized the entire ship had gone quiet. Even Captain Truxton stood quietly, giving no orders to his crew.

Then he felt it.

Like a creeping black fog, something was prying its way into his thoughts. Not something, *someone*. A woman's voice, telling him to surrender. He shook his head and tried to fight it. *Get out!* He shouted in his mind.

Looking around, he saw that the sails had gone slack. The air was still, and the ship had nearly stopped. Captain Truxton and his crew were completely mesmerized and unmoving. He shook the captain but to no avail. A shadow closed over them as the warship slowly came alongside. Grappling hooks were thrown down and attached to the side of their ship as the crew stood helplessly.

Daring pulled out his sword and prepared to defend the ship. Although certainly outnumbered, he wouldn't go without a fight. Then the voice came back, this time stronger. It soothed and calmed him, reassuring him that he didn't need his sword.

The Newcynderians laid wooden beams across the gap and swarmed over them. The Duke watched helplessly as Captain Truxton and his crew were quickly disarmed and tied up without any resistance!

A man, dressed in a blue jacket with golden epaulets on his high shoulders, stepped onto the deck. The Duke recognized the man's uniform as that of a naval officer, perhaps even a captain. The man approached Captain Truxton.

"Ah, Captain Truxton, I presume?" he said with a slight bow. "I am Admiral Barrow of the Newcynder Royal Navy. Quite delighted to meet you."

"Admiral…" Truxton's subdued voice trailed off.

"A lively chap, eh?" Admiral Barrow said jovially. "I suppose I'd be quiet, too, if I were being charged with sinking a Newcynderian merchant vessel, eh Captain?"

"Admiral," a young sailor said over his shoulder. "The queen wishes to board."

"Well, make way for her!" Admiral Barrow answered. "Make way and bow before the new queen!"

Everyone, including Captain Truxton and his crew, lowered themselves to one knee. Only Duke Daring remained standing. Then he heard her voice again. *Who are you, and why do you not kneel before me?*

You are not my queen, whoever you are. I will not kneel. He responded, in thought. Somehow, he knew she could hear him.

Kneel! The voice demanded.

The duke's legs felt weary, but he stood his ground. For some unknown reason, she did not have the same power over him as the others. A shadowy figure emerged from the warship, a woman, cloaked in elegant, black robes. He couldn't see her face, but as she held the railing, he saw her hand. On her finger was a ring with a purple orb, and although he had never seen it before, he knew whose ring it was.

"Evelyn!" he declared angrily.

Evelyn was the new queen! The spider witch who had attacked his daughters, and his kingdom, was now in charge of a royal armada! The duke's blood boiled as he looked at her, but his arms and legs seemed useless. She was protected by an aura that paralyzed any seeking to attack her.

"Can it be?" she said, looking at him, then cackling with laughter. "Admiral, do you not recognize Highcynder's greatest hero, Duke Daring?"

"My Queen," the admiral said, standing up. "THE Duke Daring? Here?"

"Yes. I wonder what Lamont would pay to get his favorite new general back," she mused.

"You knew?" the Duke said his mind racing. How could she know that?

"Oh yes, General Daring," she said. "My spies keep me well informed. I know of your new title and your mission. You haven't found them yet, have you?"

"Stay away from them!" the Duke said sternly.

"Your precious Daughters Daring will soon be joining us, as well," Evelyn said. "Admiral, take the prisoners on board and set sail for Dublari. I need to collect more slaves."

Joseph Daring sat in his room and stared at the walls. His mother had grounded him from playing outside for several days since the tiny little incident in which he set the king's ballroom on fire. Actually, it wasn't even him. It was a ball of magical energy. He wished he could get his hands on that ball now!

The sound of voices downstairs distracted him. Mother was talking to someone. He decided a little peek to see what was going on wouldn't do any harm. He crept down the hall to the top of the stairs where he saw his mother standing in the doorway.

She was talking to the baker lady, Mrs. Winterspool, or something like that. Everyone seemed to like the baker lady, but Joseph thought there was something funny about her. He caught her giving him and his sisters weird looks sometimes.

Joseph was about to go back to his room when he saw it. Just as his mother invited the baker lady in, something snuck in behind her. It was the energy ball! Mother and the baker lady hadn't seen it sneak in, but Joseph had an eye for these kinds of things! It shot under a nearby table before anyone else could notice it.

His grounding nearly forgotten, Joseph decided it was up to him to catch his sister's magic ball. This time, however, he would need something fireproof to contain it. His father's helmet would do nicely. It was all shiny metal with a leather chin strap. It sat in his father's den just past where his mother would be having tea. He would have to be sneaky.

"Can I get you some tea?" his mother asked.

Joseph almost answered before remembering she had a guest.

"Why yes, dear," Annie said. "Tea would go nicely with the pastries I brought you."

Joseph was sneaking past them and into his father's den when he heard the mention of pastries. He nearly stopped to ask for a treat, but quickly thought better of it. It was always best to ask politely if you wanted something, but if his mother were still mad at him, the answer would probably be no. Asking might not be the best option right now. He decided it would be to his advantage to borrow one when no one was looking!

As his mother and the baker lady sat down at a small table in the main room, Joseph slipped into the den and retrieved the helmet. It was a shiny helmet that he loved to wear when given the chance. He briefly thought that if he wore it, perhaps his mother wouldn't see him! After all, it was very dark inside the helmet and hard to see out of. It did make finding the magic ball of energy more difficult, but Joseph knew that all heroes had to overcome difficulties sometimes. The helmet would be his.

"Thank you, Duchess," Annie said, as she took her cup of tea. "Won't you have a pastry?"

"Well, I suppose one wouldn't hurt," Aryanna said, as she reached for a warm, flaky treat that looked to have a sweetberry filling.

Crash! Something fell to the floor in the kitchen.

"Whatever could that be?" Aryanna said. "Joseph! Are you in there?"

Of course, Joseph was not in the kitchen, he was hiding in his father's den! He watched as his mother and the baker lady's attention turned to the kitchen. When they weren't looking, the ball of energy landed right on the pastries and set them all on fire!

"What in the world?" Aryanna cried out.

"My pastries!" Annie yelled as she swatted the fire with a napkin, to no avail.

"I've never seen that happen before," Aryanna said, as she placed a large pan over the flames, extinguishing them.

"You haven't got any of those gnomes in your house, do you?" Annie asked suspiciously.

By now the magic ball had disappeared again. The two women hadn't seen it at all, but Joseph had watched it bounce up the stairs. He wasn't sure what it wanted up there, but he was sure it was up to no good!

Joseph crept up the stairs without getting caught, although he was sure he would receive the blame later. This would be twice that the meddling magic ball got him into trouble! When he reached the hallway, he noticed the ball was at Elizabeth's bedroom door. It was bumping the door and seemed insistent on getting in.

A plan sprang into his mind. Joseph decided he would open the door and trap it in Elizabeth's room. Once inside, it would be easier for him to capture it with his father's helmet. And if the magic ball were to make a mess, it was his sister's room, anyway, making his plan even better!

The magic ball paid him little attention as he opened the door, and it quickly bounced into Elizabeth's room. Joseph stepped inside and shut the door behind him. Then he removed his father's helmet. He wanted the ball to recognize him.

"I've got you, now," Joseph declared.

The magic ball continued to ignore him, though. It bounced up onto Elizabeth's desk, and from there up onto her bookshelf. It was knocking books and her collection of knickknacks and doodads all over the place! Joseph positioned himself directly under it, helmet in hands, and readied to catch it when it fell off the shelf.

Instead, he caught a pair of glasses.

And then his mother opened the door.

"Joseph Daring!" she yelled. She didn't sound happy.

Joseph instinctively hid his hands and the glasses behind his back.

"What are you doing in Elizabeth's room?" she asked. "What do you have?"

"Um, nothing." he answered quietly, looking around the room even though he knew the real culprit would be hidden.

"Show me," she said.

Joseph handed his mother the glasses. He wasn't sure exactly why he would want to keep them anyway. Joseph didn't need glasses and, come to think of it, neither did Elizabeth. He figured that the crazy magic ball needed them since it was always bumping into things.

"My, what a mess!" Annie Whipperpeel said from behind Aryanna, as she squeezed into the room. "Your son is as mischievous as his sisters!"

"My son," Aryanna said, "is my concern. Annie, do these look familiar to you?"

"Are those my old…" Annie quickly corrected herself. "Why I don't recall ever owning a pair like that, no."

"Really?" Aryanna asked. "These seem to have your initials on them."

"How strange," Annie replied. "Perhaps I lost them outside my store, and one of your children found them."

"Yes, perhaps," Aryanna said thoughtfully.

"Well, I think it's best I be going, now," Annie said. "Thank you for the tea, Duchess."

"But of course, Annie," Aryanna said with a smile. "Your visit has been most exciting!"

Joseph watched his mother walk Annie to the door and bid her farewell. After the door had been shut, Joseph heard her say something to herself.

"Exciting, and informative," she said as she cleaned up the burnt pastries.

Joseph wasn't sure what that meant. He was just glad that his mother had something else to think about other than the mess that crazy magic ball had made knocking around and catching things on fire.

"Joseph," Aryanna said. "Don't think I've forgotten about you, young man. Why don't you go back up and start cleaning the mess in Elizabeth's room."

"Yes, Mother," he said.

When he went into Elizabeth's room, the ball was in the open, seemingly waiting for him.

"I hope you're happy," he said. "This is the second time you've gotten me into trouble."

The ball just bounced up and down. It emitted a warm glow that Joseph actually found comforting.

"At least you're not catching everything on fire, now," Joseph said. "But be careful, it only takes a spark."

The ball moved in a small circle and gave a couple bounces of understanding.

"Hey! I know! I'll call you Spark!" he said to the magic ball. Spark bounced up and down in approval, then quickly bounced in circles around Joseph.

"Now," Joseph said, "what in the world am I supposed to feed you?"

STEVEN J. THOMPSON

Chapter 10

Friends in Need

The *Chainbreaker* moved slowly through the narrow channels of the Starry Isles. The misty air made it hard to see, and jagged rocks threatened from either side. The sails that weren't torn were furled so the ship could drift on the channel's current, in search of a hidden shore. Jolaia watched from the crow's nest above, although the fog was just as thick there.

Mount Cynder loomed high above them, a solid mass in the mist. It towered over them, now, like a soundless giant, defiant of the elements that clung to its base. Emily and Elizabeth had never seen a mountain so big in their lives. They stared in silence as the mist parted, then enveloped them again. The ship had come to a shore suitable for making land.

Just beyond the beach, there was a small grouping of shelters, built from little more than sticks and palm thatches. Small fire pits added a charred, smoky aroma to the dense fog. Someone was living here.

"Captain Trollbane," Emily said, "didn't you say it was uninhabited?"

"Apologies, lass," he answered. "I like to keep my secrets."

"This isn't his first slave run," Elizabeth deduced. "He's been leaving them here to start anew."

Jolaia brought the gharidian slaves, now freed, up onto the deck to show them their new home. They agreed that this seemed like a suitable place to settle. They did not want to go back to Dublari.

"Why go to all of this trouble?" Emily asked.

"So long as there are those who will make great efforts to enslave others, whether through tyranny or tax," Bartemus said, "there must always be those willing to take equal measures for the preservation of freedom. Lest someday we all end up under a master's yoke."

"What he means," Elizabeth started.

"I know what he means," Emily said, interrupting her sister as she hung her head. "And I know that I was wrong. This enslavement of others, it's evil. It's like something the spider witch would have done."

"And how do ye know tis not her work, lass?" Bartemus replied.

"Which is exactly why I brought us here," Elizabeth said, squaring herself with her older sister.

"You really think this flower you're seeking will help you against her?" Emily asked.

"I've felt a taste of its power," Elizabeth answered, patting her mother's book, "and Mother wouldn't have protected this book so well if it were filled with simple recipes for cakes and stews."

"We may yet find out if you're right," Bartemus said, "but first, we have company to deal with."

Another group of gharidians was gathering near the huts. They were armed with wooden spears and other primitive weapons that could be made on an island. Some of them seemed clearly agitated and were gesturing toward the new arrivals on their shoreline.

"Let me do the talking," Bartemus said as he and several crew members climbed over the side and into a smaller boat to take them to shore.

"Hello my friends!" he called out to them, as he reached the sand.

"Not friends," one of them said, stepping forward. The others gathered behind this one.

"But not enemies, I hope?" Bartemus asked as he cautioned his crew not to draw their weapons.

"Not enemies." the leader said. "You saved us from evil people. You left us here, with dangerous creatures."

"Dangerous creatures?" Bartemus asked. "Where?"

"They come from ruins," the leader answered, pointing inland.

"What is your name, my friend?" Bartemus asked.

"I am G'nass," the leader said.

"G'nass, I have freed more gharidians. They need a home, now."

"More to protect and feed," G'nass said. "This not help."

"What would help?" Bartemus asked.

G'nass looked around at his fellow gharidians. He looked over his shoulder at the ruins at the base of Mount Cynder. Then he looked back to Bartemus and the others.

"Stop bad creatures," G'nass said. "Then we take gharidians."

"Hail, Duchess Daring," The royal guardsman snapped to attention.

"Hello," she answered. "I am here to visit the king."

"Apologies, Duchess," he said. "The king is not well, and is not receiving guests."

"I know," she answered. "I can help. Let me through."

The royal guardsman looked at her thoughtfully then stepped aside. Not only was Duchess Daring the king's cousin, but if anyone in Highcynder could help him, it would be she. The Duchess entered the hallway to the king's personal chambers.

The curtains were drawn but not completely, letting sunlight in through the slightest crack. It illuminated the dust in the air but little else. Aryanna looked away to let her eyes adjust to the darkness.

"Your Highness?" she inquired, then saw him slumped over his desk. "Oh dear!"

"Cousin!" King Lamont coughed before he could speak again. "Do I look that bad?"

Aryanna tried her best to hide her look of concern as she pulled back the curtains and let in the light. The king was pale and haggard. His beard and hair had grown out with wisps of gray. His nails were ragged with shades of blue on the skin underneath.

"You've looked better, Your Highness," she said. "How long have you been like this? Where are your attendants?"

"I sent them away," he answered.

On the table, next to him were some baked goods. Aryanna took out a small vial of fluid and poured some on one of the pastries. It sizzled and emitted a putrid green smoke.

"What are you doing?" he asked weakly.

"The pastries," Aryanna said, frowning, "are poisoned."

"Oh, come now, Duchess!" The king said, coughing again. "Annie Whipperpeel may be annoyingly nosey, but her cooking isn't that bad!"

"I'm serious, Lamont!" she said sternly, using his given name as she handed him another vial. "Drink this. I made enough to last you several days."

"As you wish, cousin," Lamont said with a look of defeat. He did not have the strength to argue. "I shall send guards for Annie."

"Not yet," Aryanna said. "She has been working in the shadows for some time now. Let me try to find out what she's up to."

"It is she, you know," Lamont said.

"Yes, you're right," Aryanna answered, her arms crossed in worry. "This is definitely her work."

"Evelyn has returned," he said grimly.

Inside one of the thatched beach huts, Emily, Elizabeth, and Jolaia were standing around a table examining a crude map of the island.

"Good, you're back," Elizabeth said, as Bartemus and Gaeron joined them.

"What have you learned?" Emily asked.

"Only that the creatures are living in the ruins and attack the gharidians at night," Gaeron said.

"What kind of creatures are they?" Elizabeth asked.

"The undead," Bartemus said. "Skeletons. 'Tis not clear what animates them."

"When I was younger," Gaeron began, "the elves told tales of an ancient city beneath Mount Cynder. Its people were intelligent and advanced, but their hunger for knowledge corrupted them. They turned to dark arts to unlock the secrets of the world. It is said that one of them, a great wizard, unleashed the evil power of necromancy onto the world. With his great power, he claimed the throne. But he doomed his people, and cursed them with the eternal life of the undead."

"And you still left the gharidians here?" Emily asked.

"They were just stories," Bartemus insisted, putting his hands up defensively.

"Which now we know are true," Gaeron said, his hand on Bartemus' shoulder. "We need to make it right, my captain."

"Agreed," Bartemus said with a sigh. "But I can't endanger these lasses."

"We accept the danger," Emily said.

"And there's no way we're staying behind," Elizabeth added. "You can let us help you, or I will go there alone if need be."

"Still as stubborn as your father," Bartemus said. "I suppose it's settled then. You can go with us. You may yet wish you hadn't."

Everyone went silent as Bartemus looked around at them.

"Everyone, make preparations — weapons, torches, and cloth for bandages."

"Bandages?" Emily asked apprehensively.

"These aren't goblins we be facing, lass," Bartemus answered. "Prepare yourselves. We leave soon."

"You should wait until morning," a small voice said.

They all turned to see a young gharidian in the doorway. The gharidian girl was holding a carved wooden doll, and Emily and Elizabeth were both reminded of their little brother Joseph. The gharidian walked over to a straw nest in the corner of the hut and made herself comfortable.

"Why should we wait until morning, little one?" Elizabeth asked.

"It'll be dark soon, and the monsters mostly come at night," she answered. "Mostly."

As darkness settled over the gharidian village, another ship drifted quietly through the channel. There were no lanterns on the deck, just darkness, and an eerie silence. The captain worried about damaging his ship but was warned to do as he was told.

"What do you see, brother?" Jefferson Black whispered as loud as he dare.

"Adjust to port," Gordon replied. "Then straight."

Although Gordon was more rogue than a sailor, his night vision surpassed that of anyone else on board. Jefferson trusted that his adopted half-brother would get them through the channel safely. Whether or not they would successfully sneak up on the dwarf was another matter, but they were both good at sneaking, too.

"Stop here," Gordon whispered.

The crew quietly lowered the anchor and moored the ship. The water here was shallow and protected by the towering rocks on either side. Jefferson looked up at the sky but could only see the thick fog, and the red peak of Mount Cynder. He had to wonder why anyone would have named this place the Starry Isles.

Gordon was already securing his gear. He tied the end of his two-handed sword to his waist. Then Gordon put some other tools and supplies in a burlap sack. Finally, he tied his hair back in a ponytail.

"Stay out of sight of the other ship," Jefferson told the captain, "and wait for our return."

"I had better be paid extra for this," the captain said.

"The new queen will pay a hefty ransom for the prisoners we seek," Jefferson said. "She'll also be extremely disappointed should this mission fail. I trust you do not wish to disappoint her?"

"No," the captain responded quickly. "Of course not!"

"Then be sure you are ready for departure on our return," Jefferson said.

With that, Jefferson and Gordon slipped over the side of the ship and lowered themselves down into the water. The captain could barely hear them swimming away in the darkness, and then they were gone. Assigning two crew members to the watch, he retired to his quarters to settle in for the night.

STEVEN J. THOMPSON

Chapter 11

The Banshee's Scream

Elizabeth read through her mother's book one last time, memorizing the description and location of the flower she sought. It was exciting to know that she was finally close to finding it. The lone candle in the room, brought with them from their ship, allowed for her and the others to prepare and await their quest.

"So, do you think you'll find it?" Emily asked as she and Jolaia sharpened their swords.

"This is the only place where it is known to grow," Elizabeth answered.

"Why does it grow here?" Emily asked.

"I don't think you want to know," Elizabeth said with a wry grin.

"Oh come on, tell me." Emily prodded.

"Very well." Elizabeth sighed. "It grows here, under the slopes of Mount Cynder, because of a critical fertilizer that can only be found here, as well."

"Fertilizer?" Emily asked.

"Yes," Elizabeth continued. "Not just any fertilizer. Harpy dung."

"Harpy, eeew!" Emily squealed. "That's gross! And you want to eat these flowers that grow in it?"

"No, not eat them," Elizabeth said matter-of-factly. "Just grind them into a potion that I can drink."

Emily and Jolaia gave each other a look of disgust. Elizabeth had noticed the two becoming fast friends and was glad for her sister. It hadn't been her intention to bring Emily along, but it gave her a lot of comfort that she was here. At least Emily had gained something from the journey.

"This potion," Emily asked, "does it make you more powerful? Like before?"

"Yes," Elizabeth answered. "It amplifies my magical energy — fills me up with it. It was rather, exhilarating."

"But it's dangerous," Emily said. "You struggled to control it. And you've risked our lives coming here for it! Liz, don't you see the danger in that?"

"I'm not asking you to understand me, Em," Elizabeth said with her hands on her hips. "We were powerless when the spider witch had us in her lair! But she showed me what real power is, and I can't just ignore it while our family is in danger. I'm not turning back."

"So what else is in this book, Elizabeth Daring?" Jolaia asked, changing the subject.

"What else?" Elizabeth answered. "I suppose I focused on the flower. There's a chapter about crystals, though, and, a small section on unicorns."

"Unicorns?" Emily asked, her eyes lighting up. "I would love to see one! Why couldn't we have searched for those, instead?"

"Because, unicorns do not amplify magic," Elizabeth started, "they nullify it."

"Is everyone ready?" Bartemus asked as he stepped inside. He had gone back to the ship to retrieve climbing ropes.

"Elizabeth," Gaeron said, handing her a short, white staff. "I want you to take this. It has the power that will help ward off the evils we might face."

"Thank you, Gaeron," Elizabeth said. "I trust you have one for yourself?"

Gaeron hefted another, taller staff and nodded. The one he carried had intricate carvings, and the handle was wrapped in fine leather. A strange rock was fastened to the end. Even as he held it near her, Elizabeth could feel the magical power emanating from it.

"If we are all fully equipped," Bartemus said impatiently, "G'nass is waiting to guide us to the ruins. It is time, my friends."

A solemn quiet hung over the five adventurers as they left the thatched hut. Bartemus walked in front. He was garbed in chain mail and a polished half helmet that gleamed in the moonlight. He carried a dwarven axe in both hands and a pair of handcrafted daggers on his belt. On his back was a short, wooden crossbow that looked to have seen numerous adventures.

Jolaia and Emily followed him. Jolaia had donned a light leather armor that provided protection but still allowed some freedom of movement. On her sides, she carried a pair of curved Dublari blades. Emily had, instead, chosen a single sword with a brass handguard that reminded her of her father's sword. On her left arm, she had strapped a light buckler for protection.

Elizabeth and Gaeron brought up the rear, both carrying magic staves and a small arsenal of potions and salves on their waists. Gaeron also had several magical scrolls tucked into his belt. Still not sure of her magical prowess, Elizabeth longed for her bow and arrows, as well. All of them carried packs with extra gear, food, and medical supplies.

G'nass alone met them at the edge of the village. The other gharidians had taken shelter for the night, but he had agreed to get them to the ruins. Beyond that, they would be on their own. He led them on a sandy path beneath an ever-thickening canopy of trees. It was warm and muggy here, and the buzzing of scores of insects was almost deafening. Emily pulled at the neck of her leather cuirass as she sweated underneath.

The path twisted deeper into the jungle until they could no longer see the stars for the trees above. The air became hot and sweltering, making everyone sweat beneath their armor and robes. The foliage was also thick and constantly seemed to grab them. The path, however, remained untouched. It was as though nothing living could grow on it.

Finally, they came to a pair of enormous stone pillars that reached up beyond the trees. Covered in vines, Elizabeth could just make out carved symbols on their surfaces. There were more pillars beyond them. The air was still, but much cooler than the humid jungle behind them.

"I stop here," G'nass said, as he made a fist and put it across his chest in a salute to Bartemus.

"Thank you, my friend," Bartemus said, returning the gesture. "We will find the source of this evil and end it for you."

"What exactly are we looking for?" Emily whispered to Elizabeth.

"All dark magic has a source," Gaeron said. "A curse that lasts a significant amount of time must usually be bound to an earthen object."

"And how will we find it?" Emily asked.

"Magic resonates with those who wield it," Gaeron explained. "Your sister and I will be able to feel it as we get closer."

"And how will the rest of us know?" Emily asked.

"We'll know," Bartemus said, "because that's where the monsters will likely be."

"True," Gaeron said, "that is where the danger will also be the greatest."

Bartemus hushed them all and lit their torches. He motioned for them to use the hand signals he had taught them back in the village. He then made them follow ten paces behind. If there were traps, he was the most equipped to find and either disarm or evade them.

As they traveled into the ruins, they were amazed at the giant columns of stone that towered over them. The effects of centuries of weather and erosion could be seen, but entire buildings still stood silently throughout the ancient city. Some were completely covered in foliage, trees had grown through some, while others still were oddly untouched by any sign of life at all.

Bartemus motioned for them to stop as he investigated something moving up ahead. Jolaia rested her hands on the handles of her blades, ready to quickly slide them from their scabbards. Elizabeth just tried to breathe as quietly as possible and listened.

There were no sounds to be heard. Where the jungle had been full of life, here, it was deathly quiet, save for the fluttering of their torches. Bartemus gave them the signal to advance.

And then a woman's scream - loud like the scream of a hundred women - pierced the silence and echoed through the night. It was followed by the sound of footsteps running toward them. Footsteps, and the clattering of ancient weapons.

"You hear that?" Gordon Black turned and asked Jefferson, his massive two-handed sword hefted in front of him.

"Yes, I'm sure the whole island did," Jefferson said. "We're still going in there."

"Safer to wait here?" Gordon tried.

"Not for our quarry, brother," Jefferson answered. "The queen wants them alive, so bolster up and let's get this over with. Not afraid are you?"

Gordon growled and turned back to the giant stone pillars leading into the ancient city. His green-hued muscles bulging out from under his leather tunic made the half-orc a fearsome sight. But even Gordon could feel that these ruins were not safe for a mortal, living beings like himself and Jefferson. He gripped his sword tighter and stepped forward into the city.

"Skeletons!" Bartemus yelled as he hefted his axe in the air.

A small group of ancient skeletons was running their way. Dust and cobwebs still hung from their bones and patches of armor they wore. Their jawbones gaped up and down, as if they were silently communicating with each other, or sadly trying to. Their bony feet clicked on the cobblestones as they ran forward carrying swords, spears, and whatever various weapons they seemed able to find.

The first skeleton reached Bartemus ahead of the others and was quickly cleaved in two. Behind it came several more, armed with swords, spears, and even shields. Jolaia was the first to reach the dwarf's side as her curved blades spun into action. Emily came up behind her and guarded her flank. They were at an intersection of four paths coming together between the ancient buildings. The first skeletons had originated from the west, and more foes could already be heard coming from the east.

Elizabeth could feel her staff begin to hum with energy as if it could feel the presence of evil and longed to unleash its power. She raised it in front of her as three skeletons rounded a corner to the east. The staff glowed brightly, and an intense white light burst from its tip. The skeletons were obliterated.

Jolaia dispatched two more skeletons, and Emily slashed her sword at another, but in cleaving the skeleton's arm her sword lodged in its ribcage, trapping her as it flailed with its free hand. Emily used her buckler to deflect its wild blows until she could pull the sword free and kick the creature away from her. It looked up at her with hollow eye sockets and came at her again, but this time she slashed its head from its shoulders, and it fell motionless.

"Is that," Emily panted, "the last of them?"

"It is for now," Bartemus answered.

"What was that scream?" Jolaia asked, still brandishing her swords.

"Most likely a banshee," Gaeron answered. "And it's still out there."

"A banshee?" Emily asked.

"Yes," Gaeron said. "The powerful spirit of a former witch. Legend has it they can control the undead."

Almost in answer, the night was pierced by a second scream, this time louder than the first. They held their hands over their ears as it echoed throughout the ancient city. Finally, it faded. And then there was movement around them.

"Look!" Elizabeth pointed.

The bones of the skeletons they had defeated started pulling back together, reclaiming their original forms. Somehow, the banshee's scream was reanimating them.

"We cannot keep this up," Bartemus said. "We need shelter."

They ran farther north up the ancient road, dispatching several smaller groups of skeletons along the way. Each group they defeated almost immediately began rebuilding themselves until a small army could be heard marching behind them in the darkness.

Finally, they came upon a large stone structure built into the base of Mount Cynder. Level after level of the building towered above them, reaching a broad plateau carved into the mountain. An eerie light shone from the windows of the highest room.

"There," Gaeron said, pointing at the windows. "Elizabeth, do you feel it?"

"Yes," Elizabeth answered. "My staff is humming again."

"That is the source," Gaeron said.

"Then we need to get inside," Bartemus declared. "But the entrance is blocked!"

Although the structure was still sound, an enormous stone slab blocked the only doorway. Bartemus and Gaeron tried pushing, but it was too heavy. Worse, more skeletons were approaching.

"We're trapped," Bartemus said grimly, as he readied his axe.

A battle cry rang out as a giant sword cut through two skeletons from behind. They watched in awe as a large figure spun again, cutting down several more. Still more approached, but these were blown apart by a glowing, magical missile that hurtled into them.

"What is this?" Bartemus said, holding up a torch.

Two figures approached them and stepped into the light, one noticeably bigger than the other.

"Hello there!" the robed one called out. "I am Jefferson Black, and this is my brother Gordon."

"What is your business here?" Bartemus asked, trying to make out their faces.

"Apparently the business of saving you," Jefferson replied snidely.

"We don't need saving," Bartemus said. "Have we met, sorcerer?"

"I don't think so," Jefferson answered. "We were commissioned by King Lamont to find the Daughters Daring."

"The king sent you?" Emily exclaimed. "Where is our father?"

"Searching for you, as well, I'm sure," Jefferson answered, then gave Bartemus a quizzical look. "Although likely not in an ancient city cursed with the undead."

"A story for later," Bartemus replied.

"If there is a later," Gaeron interjected. "More skeletons are approaching."

This time the army was larger. Emily could see at least thirty of them marching in an orderly formation. An apparition of a woman floated in the air behind them, her white hair flowing as if in water, her face contorted in an eternal scream.

"The banshee?" Elizabeth asked.

"Yes," Gaeron answered, preparing a spell.

Emily and Jolaia brandished swords and took a fighting stance. Gordon snorted and bared his tusks as he stepped toward the approaching enemies, only stopping when Jefferson laid a hand on his shoulder.

"Brother, the slab," Jefferson said.

Nodding, Gordon turned to the great rock slab blocking the doorway. His muscles strained as he pushed with all of his might, but the plate was barely moving. Bartemus joined in to help, but it was still too heavy. Gaeron turned to help, as well, but Jefferson stopped him.

"Guard our backs," Jefferson said. "I will assist them."

Gaeron nodded and turned back to help the girls who had now formed a line of defense. Swords in the front, spells in the back. Jefferson faced the slab and sat down on the ground. He closed his eyes and began to concentrate. It started to move.

"It's working!" Bartemus yelled. "Keep pushing!"

Behind them, Emily Daring cried out in pain. One of the skeletons had cut her shoulder above her buckler, and she fell back. Elizabeth stepped forward and fought them back with her staff. Making matters worse, the skeletons were behaving more like trained, organized soldiers, now. Each one they defeated seemed only to come back even stronger, and smarter.

Standing alone, Jolaia gave a fierce battle cry and sprang into action. She spun in circles, her twin blades whirling around at extreme speeds, cutting through skeletons and breaking them into dusty piles of bones. When they closed in on her, she leaped into the air, flipping over and landing behind them where she slashed them to pieces. The others could only watch in awe as the sword maiden carried out her deadly dance of blades.

Gordon watched in awe, as well. With the slab now moved, he had turned to join the battle only to see it wasn't necessary. The girl in front of him was as deadly as she was beautiful, and he found a strange tightness in his chest he had never felt before.

"Gordon!" Jefferson yelled, snapping him out of his trance. "Cover our flank! Get everyone inside, then we'll block the entrance again!"

Bartemus took up his torch and went inside first, followed by Elizabeth helping Emily along with Jefferson and Gaeron guarding the rear. Gordon had joined Jolaia in a slashing frenzy of steel and bone. Together they were the perfect fighting pair — his large swing alongside her precise attacks. But no matter how many they cut down, more continued to join the battle.

"Get inside!" Gaeron shouted. "I will hold them off!"

The last two ran into the building as Gaeron pulled a scroll from a pouch in his robe. As he began reading it, the letters on the paper ignited in bright light, almost burning off the paper. Elizabeth could see the aura of power surrounding him as he cited the incantation. When the last words were read a great wall of fire erupted just outside the doorway, blocking the skeleton army from reaching them. Some tried to enter but were instantly incinerated.

"I'll take it from here," Jefferson said as he focused again on the stone slab, sliding it inch-by-inch back in front of the entrance.

"Well, now they can't get in here," Emily said as she winced in pain from her shoulder wound.

"And we can't get out either," Elizabeth said between breaths as she applied salve and a bandage on her sister's wound.

"Nonsense," Bartemus said as he scanned the room with his torch. "I've been in worse scrapes than this. We'll find a way out just fine after we've dealt with the source of this cursed place!"

"I would suggest," Gaeron said, pointing to a dark stone stairway leading up. "That we start there."

"We will," Bartemus said, then turned to Jefferson and Gordon. "But first, I would know more of you two. I do not believe you are brothers, and you are more likely the queen's spies than agents of King Lamont!"

Gordon bared his teeth and stepped forward, brandishing his sword. He stopped short when Jolaia met him halfway, her own swords extended toward him. The two stayed squared off for a moment, until Jefferson stepped forward.

"Brother, please." He said with a hand on Gordon's shoulder. "And my brother he is, though not of birth. We were raised together since childhood."

"That does not explain your presence here, sorcerer!" Bartemus replied.

"As I said earlier, we were sent by King Lamont," Jefferson answered calmly. "When the Daughters Daring went missing, the king offered a great reward for their safe return. My brother and I are soldiers of fortune if you will, and never pass up a paying job."

"We could certainly use their help," Gaeron said.

"Very well," Bartemus said, lowering his axe. "Help us end the curse on this island, and I will personally see to it that you receive your reward."

"What other choice do we have?" Jefferson answered. "Of course we will help."

"But be warned, Brothers Black," Bartemus added, "do not cross me. I'll be watching you both."

Bartemus headed up the dark stairway, followed by the others. Gordon was still standing across from Jolaia, who gave him a wink as she turned to follow the others. His face flushed momentarily, and then he took up the rear behind his brother as they ascended into the tower.

Chapter 12
Evil's Source

Aryanna Daring approached the chambers of the Knights Council. It was almost time for the meeting, but the room was oddly quiet. A few hushed conversations could be heard, but not the unruly ruckus she had witnessed before.

"Ah, Duchess Daring," Baron Ocwen said, "you've arrived." He was seated in the head chair.

"Indeed I have, Baron Ocwen," she answered. "Where is Duke Archibald?"

"He was feeling ill, dearie," Annie Whipperpeel chimed in. "But not to worry. I sent him home with some of my treats to help lift his spirits!"

"I see," Aryanna answered quietly. She knew something was amiss.

"Duchess," Baron Ocwen said. "Now that you have arrived, there is a most unpleasant matter I feel we should discuss."

"What would that be?"

"Word has arrived about your husband," Ocwen said. "I'm afraid his ship was captured by the Newcynder Navy."

"Captured?" Aryanna asked. "Why would they capture one of our ships? What are the charges?"

"The attack and destruction of a Newcynder trade vessel," Ocwen answered solemnly.

"He would never!" Aryanna exclaimed. She looked around the room, but the faces there showed no signs of support. Baron Ocwen controlled them, now.

"I'm afraid it is true," Ocwen said. "An act such as this could invite war. I'm afraid we have no choice but to leave Duke Daring to his fate."

"Cowards!" Aryanna exclaimed. "You would leave my daughters to their fate, as well! If the Knights Council does not offer help, I will discuss this with the king."

"Given the king's health," Ocwen said, "we do not feel that would be wise."

On the baron's words, two guards approached Aryanna and took hold of her.

"Take your hands off of me!" Aryanna said. "You have no authority to do this."

"Duchess," Ocwen said, standing and puffing out his chest, "you and your son may yet be the last of a family of Highcynder's greatest heroes. You are to be escorted to your home where you will be safely watched over. It is in the best interest of everyone."

"This is not in Highcynder's best interest, or my family's," Aryanna said, her shoulders square.

"Be that as it may," Ocwen said, "it is our decision. Guards, please escort the Duchess to Daring Manor and ensure that she is kept comfortable there."

The guards escorted a solemn Duchess Daring out of the council chamber. As they walked down the street to her home, they failed to see several small figures scurrying behind the hedges. The gnomes watched as the guards passed, before stepping into the open.

"Wasn't that the duchess?" one of them asked.

"Yes, it was," Randolph said. "And she didn't seem happy with her company."

"Then we should rescue her!" the other gnome said.

"We will," Randolph said. "But first, we need help. It's time we call an audience with the faerie folk."

The stairway was tight and narrow, forcing the adventurers to advance single file. Bartemus took the lead as he had experience in spotting and disarming any traps. The others followed with Gordon in the back. The half-orc grunted several times as he had to hunch and squeeze through the narrow passage.

Fortunately, they found few attackers on the way, save for a few random skeletons that were dispatched with ease. They could hear the clattering of the skeletal army from below, along with the banshee's wailing. If they did not find the source of the evil in this building, Elizabeth feared they would be trapped there for a long time.

"This is it!" Bartemus called down to them. "The highest floor!"

They ascended onto a sprawling terrace which stretched around the face of the mountain. There, ornate, but rusty, doors led to a great hall and throne room. The outer terrace was weathered and covered in dust. Weeds and foliage grew in the corners. Emily peered over the edge to see that the skeleton army was still waiting below.

Bartemus and Gordon pried open the doors to the great hall. Dusty tapestries and jeweled decorations lined the walls. Ancient chairs faced inward and created an aisle to a throne at the head of the room. A tall skeleton, covered in webs and dust, sat on the throne, with bony fingers on an ancient sword. The skeleton's crown glowed with an eerie light.

"Once a great king," Jefferson said with a sneer. "Now just a dusty skeleton. At least he left us some treasures, eh?"

"Elizabeth," Gaeron said, nodding at the crown. "Do you feel it?"

"Yes," she answered. "That's the source?"

"Indeed it is," Jefferson said, reaching for it. "Looks valuable, too. Let's take it and be done with this!"

"No, wait!" Gaeron shouted, too late.

As Jefferson's fingers touched the crown, a pulse of light shot out of it. He collapsed to the floor as energy flowed out of him and into the skeleton. The huge frame shook its head, and dust puffed out from its toothy jaws. It was coming back to life.

"What happened?" Bartemus shouted from behind them.

"It's some kind of lich!" Gaeron answered. "It feeds on the essence of the living!"

Gordon roared in anger with his sword above his head and rushed the skeleton king, only to be flung against the wall by a bolt of dark energy. Jefferson continued to writhe in agony on the floor, as Gordon watched helplessly.

Elizabeth held up her staff and focused her will. Beams of light shot out, disrupting the energy that held and drained Jefferson. The skeleton king looked at her now, weighing the power of his young adversary. He then called out a powerful enchantment in an ancient language but was interrupted by a crossbow bolt to the mouth.

"Ye'll not be calling for help, dark one," Bartemus yelled, as he reloaded his crossbow.

"Too late!" Emily announced as she looked over the side of the balcony at the skeleton army that was now climbing the mountain wall. "They're coming!" she yelled. "We have to finish this!"

Jolaia and Bartemus attacked with swords and axe. The skeleton king parried their blows and swung wildly with his sword, smashing chairs and tables behind them. While he chased them around the room, Elizabeth and Gaeron helped Jefferson to his feet.

"He was stealing my life force!" Jefferson said weakly.

"Help me hold him back!" Gaeron said, to Jefferson. "Elizabeth, your staff can defeat him!"

The skeleton king knocked Bartemus away and pushed Jolaia into a corner. It was too tight for her to maneuver, and her swords weren't hurting him. She tried to spin past him, but he caught her with the hilt of his sword, knocking her back into the wall. He laughed as he raised his sword over her.

Gordon advanced again, bringing his massive sword down on the skeleton king's shoulder, cutting off the arm. The ancient sword clanged to the ground as he spun around, grabbing Gordon by the throat with his remaining arm, and uttering menacingly in his ancient language. His very touch was draining the half orc's life force. With incredible strength, he tossed Gordon on top of Jolaia, dazing them both.

"We've got company!" Emily shouted. She had taken up Bartemus' crossbow and was firing bolts into the climbing skeletons, who were now only a floor below them. "Hurry!"

"Now!" Gaeron shouted as he unleashed a fire spell onto the skeleton king. Standing beside him, Jefferson unleashed a spell of arcing electricity. The combination scorched their enemy. For a moment, the skeleton king wavered. His bones were smoking and charred, and he seemed to be lifeless. The room had gone silent.

Elizabeth ran to Emily's side. "Are they still coming?" she asked.

In answer, a bony hand reached over the top of the brick wall of the terrace. Emily brought the butt of her crossbow down on its wrist, breaking it off and sending the skeleton plummeting.

"Does that answer your question?" Emily said, nearly breathless and clutching her wounded shoulder.

"Look out!" Gaeron shouted as the skeleton king returned to life. It sent a shock wave into Gaeron and Jefferson, knocking them both into the wall, unconscious.

The skeleton king then turned his attention to Emily and Elizabeth. They were the only ones left standing, and they were mere children, but he was wary of Elizabeth's staff.

"He's scared of you!" Emily said to her sister.

"No," Elizabeth answered, wanting to run but seeing no escape. "He's too powerful, and I can't control it."

"Liz, you can stop him!" Emily said, putting her arm over her sister's shoulder. "I'm with you."

Her courage bolstered by her sister, Elizabeth focused on her staff, and a blinding white light emanated from it. It illuminated the hall, lighting the once darkened corners like the sun itself. The skeleton king cringed and sought retreat, but there was nowhere for him to hide. His dark essence seeping out of him as the light burned it away. Elizabeth focused harder, and the light coalesced into one bright beam, which she focused on the skeleton king.

The beam of light was too bright for anyone to look at, and Elizabeth thought her hands would burn as she held the staff. But she held on, and the beam of pure white light shot into the skeleton king. Emily closed her eyes but held on tight to her sister. The light poured out of the throne room into the night sky, illuminating the ancient city below.

And with a final flash, it was gone.

Jolaia was the first to awaken. She rolled Gordon's stout frame off of her as gently as she could. The half-orc seemed brutish, but he had come to her rescue more than once this night. She pondered this for a moment, then went to Bartemus and woke him.

"The Daring Girls," Bartemus said, rubbing his head, "where are they?"

Jolaia looked around. The Daughters Daring were gone. A pile of scorched bones and dust lay on the floor where the skeleton king had once stood. His jeweled crown, its light now gone, lay nearby. Beneath them, the city lay in silent darkness. The Banshee could be heard no more.

"They can't have gone far," Jolaia answered. "We'll find them, once we tend to the others here."

"That won't be necessary," Jefferson Black said, standing next to Gordon. "We will find them and escort them home. I suggest you stay out of our way."

"Brigand!" Bartemus exclaimed. "I knew something was amiss with you!"

Bartemus and Jolaia brandished their weapons and circled around their two foes. But Bartemus' back was to the parapet, and he realized his mistake too late. Jefferson lashed out with a blast of energy that sent Bartemus flying out into the darkness of the night and falling to his certain doom.

"No!" Jolaia screamed as she ran to the terrace wall to look for him in vain. There was only darkness.

Fighting off tears, she turned and launched her attack, spanning the distance between herself and Jefferson with incredible speed. Her sword came down inches from Jefferson's neck but was blocked by Gordon's own sword. Furiously, she slashed at Gordon, high and low, over and over. The half-orc parried her blows, even taking some cuts to his arms, but was reluctant to strike her. He backed away as she pressed her attack.

Jefferson lashed out with his electricity spell, shocking her back into unconsciousness. Gordon caught her as she fell, and laid her gently on the floor.

"Gordon!" Jefferson yelled furiously. "What was that? Do you fancy her?"

Gordon glared back at Jefferson and bared his tusks. He then looked Jolaia over for burns and brushed her hair from her face.

"She is not our mission," Jefferson said. "We must find the Daughters Daring and leave this cursed place at once!"

"Elizabeth!" Emily exclaimed. "We have to leave here! Where are you going?"

Elizabeth was up ahead of Emily, both carrying torches as they made their way around the side of the mountain. Elizabeth had found a trail leading off of the terrace and up the mountain. She was certain she would find the elusive flower she treasured. Her mother's book was in her pack, ready, should she need to refer to its pages.

"Emily, calm down," Elizabeth answered. "We're just going for a little stroll while the others recuperate. They're in no danger anymore."

"But we might be," Emily said. "Didn't you say there were harpies on this mountain?"

"Well, technically, yes," Elizabeth admitted. "One couldn't very well find a flower that grows in harpy dung without first having a few harpies around!"

"Ugh," Emily said with a shiver. "Liz, don't harpies eat people?"

"Quiet," Elizabeth said. "What's this?"

Up ahead there was an outcropping of rocks above the trail. Underneath the rocks was a small grove of flora. Elizabeth pulled out her mother's book to check the description of her desired flower.

"Yes!" Elizabeth declared with excitement. "That's it!" There are several growing here!"

Elizabeth took out a small pouch and carefully began picking the magical flowers. Emily noticed that the small grove had a pretty foul smell to it.

"Eew," Emily said. "Liz, I think those rocks are a perch!"

"Hmm?" Elizabeth peered upward. "Oh yes, you're quite right. We should be going soon, then."

They suddenly heard the sound of large wings overhead as something approached in the night sky. They could hear talons clicking and scratching on the rocks above. Emily looked at Elizabeth and put her finger up to her lips. They realized too late that their torches gave them away.

"Who is there?" A crackly voice said from above. "We see your light. Who are you?"

Emily put her hand on her sword, but Elizabeth cautioned her against it. Instead, she held up her staff.

STEVEN J. THOMPSON

"We are the Daughters Daring," Elizabeth said. "We mean you no harm."

"No harm you say?" the creature answered. "And what, youngling, will you say if we decide to harm you?"

"Then we will defend ourselves," Elizabeth yelled back. "But then you will not receive our gift!"

"A gift?" the voice crackled. "What gift is this?"

Emily looked up to see a large wing unfolding above the rocks. She briefly saw what looked like an old woman, with feathers instead of hair. She gripped her sword tightly, ready for an attack.

"We have vanquished the curse on the ancient city below," Elizabeth said. "The undead will plague you no longer. To ensure this, I will give you the magic staff that ended the evil magic."

The harpies above seemed to be conferring with each other. The mountain air was cold, and Emily was trying to keep her teeth from chattering while watching the harpies in case they attacked.

"You have our gratitude for lifting the curse." the voice said. "What do you want in return for this gift?"

"Safe passage for our party," Elizabeth said. "And a peaceful union between your kind and the gharidians who live below. They prefer the shoreline to your mountains, and will not bring you trouble."

Again the harpies seemed to be speaking to each other in a strange, chirping language.

"We accept your terms, Daughters Daring," the harpy said. "You may go, but your auras suggest a dark fate ahead of you. Much difficulty and even suffering. Perhaps it would be more merciful for us to keep you here and simply eat you?"

Emily reached for her sword again, this time in anger, but Elizabeth stopped her again.

"A kind offer," Elizabeth said. "But we choose to make our own fate, and if you eat us, the curse may yet return."

"Very well," the harpy said. "We will honor this pact. You may go. Take these feathers as a sign of our respect."

Elizabeth placed the staff on the ground as two harpy feathers floated down to them. They retrieved the feathers and made their way back down the trail. The first light of morning was starting to show, and they didn't want to worry their companions any longer.

"Elizabeth, how did you know the harpies wouldn't attack us?" Emily asked.

"I read about them, of course," Elizabeth answered. "Harpies aren't very nice, but they respect pacts and magic. I was pretty sure they would honor our bargain because we lifted that curse."

"Pretty sure?" Emily asked, raising an eyebrow.

"What can I say?" Elizabeth said, laughing. "I bluffed a little!"

"That's what I thought," Emily said. "Hey, is Periwinkle in your backpack? He's been awfully quiet."

"No, he isn't. But I did see him rummaging in Bartemus' pack earlier before we left the village."

"That little scoundrel deserted us for a knapsack with more food?" Emily said, jokingly.

"Emily," Elizabeth said, "something's wrong."

When they rounded the corner back onto the terrace overlooking the city, Emily saw Gaeron and Jolaia first. Both were bound and gagged. Gordon Black stood in front of them.

"What is this?" Emily shouted as she drew her sword, not waiting for Elizabeth's caution this time. "What have you..."

Emily Daring slumped to the floor, deeply asleep. Elizabeth looked around and saw Jefferson Black in the shadows. He had cast a sleep spell, but apparently had not the energy left to cast it on two people. Her hands came up in front of her, the words of her fire spell on the edge of her lips.

"Think carefully, Elizabeth," Jefferson said, his hands up reflexively. "You cannot fight us both. If you cast that fire spell at Gordon, you may burn your friends. If you cast it at me, he will be on you in seconds. Your only option is surrender."

"Surrender? Who are you? And where is Bartemus?" Elizabeth said, not lowering her hands.

"Bartemus is dead, Elizabeth," Jefferson replied. "He fell off the ledge behind you. Now surrender, or the elf mage goes next!"

"Very well then," she said, lowering her hands. She was outnumbered and had no other option. "I will come with you."

Jefferson bound Elizabeth's wrists together and escorted her toward the stairs. Gordon lifted Emily over his shoulder and followed. He looked back, just before walking down the narrow stairway, to look at Jolaia one last time. His head hung low as he realized she would never trust him, and always see him as an enemy.

"Come along, Gordon," Jefferson called out from below. "We have a ship to catch."

As Jefferson and Gordon Black left the tower and made their way through the ancient city, they failed to see a dwarf, hanging from a tree that had grown up through one of the collapsed buildings. Long silk ropes attached at his waist and shoulders dangled him from the branches above. Bartemus watched as the Brothers Black escorted the Daughters Daring away.

"Brigands," Bartemus said as he spat angrily. "I will find you and free them."

He looked up at the tree limbs holding his parachute, which wasn't about to budge. Looking down, he realized that it was still a far drop to the ground below. Perhaps not a fatal fall, but it would hurt.

"Now," he said, "how do I get down from here?"

"Down you say?" A little voice said from behind him.

"Who's back there?" Bartemus exclaimed.

"It's me! Periwinkle the garden gnome, at your service! Or perhaps, I should say, my own service. I'm afraid I went through most of your food rations earlier, which made me quite sleepy. So I decided to take just the smallest little nap. But then I felt myself falling, FALLING! Can you believe it? And then, I woke up here! Quite the adventure if I do say so myself."

"Please," Bartemus pleaded, "do not say any more. Just help me get down from here."

"Ah yes, down," Periwinkle answered, pulling a blade from the backpack. "This ought to do the trick!

And with a quick slice of the silken cords, Bartemus and Periwinkle found themselves falling. Again. Bartemus had been right. The fall wasn't lethal, but it did hurt. He lay there, groaning, for a few moments. Then stood up and brushed himself off.

"Now," Bartemus said, shielding his eyes from the morning sun, "time to collect the others, and go save our friends."

The End

PLEASE, leave a review!

Authors really depend on your reviews to help us improve our craft and market our work. Think of it like leaving a tip.

Stay tuned for the final chapter of the Daughters Daring series as Emily, Elizabeth and even Joseph, have more exciting adventures:

The Daughters Daring & the Unicorn's Song

Other works in this series include:

The Daughters Daring
& The Enchanted Forest

Find out about more of my books on: Facebook or AMAZON

Thank you for reading

The Daughters Daring

& The Crystal Sea!

Character Profiles

Emily Daring: The oldest daughter. Brave, athletic, and compassionate. Emily is growing now, perhaps too fast in her father's eyes. She enjoys swordplay and the fame that comes with saving a kingdom. But she worries for her sister and has lessons yet to learn.

Elizabeth Daring: Faced with her own fears, Elizabeth craves knowledge and magical power. Wise beyond her years, but her quest endangers those around her. Will she attain what she seeks, or bring her family to disaster?

Joseph Daring: The Daughters' younger brother. Joseph's curiosity leads him on adventures of his own.

Duke Daring: The Hero of Highcynder, Duke Daring worries still about his daughters' safety, and over Emily's newfound interest in a boy. The King hopes that the Duke will help lead their people through troubled times.

Duchess Daring: Mother to the Daring children and favored cousin of King Lamont. Her magical abilities go back to her connection with the faeries, but she also has a history with Evelyn, the spider queen. She believes firmly in a new direction for their country while taking care of her family.

Periwinkle: A garden gnome who is much smaller than his forest cousins, Periwinkle now enjoys living with the Daring family, as long they keep him fed.

Brig Baysong: Highcynder's Dockmaster and old boat-hand. Little goes on in the port that Brig doesn't know about. He gets his chance to go back on the ocean when the daughters slip past his watchful eye.

Baron Ocwen: A member of the Knights Council, the baron's friendly guise hides his secret treachery. As Highcynder's first noble to own slaves, his presence is corrupting. But Emily Daring finds his son, Tobias Ocwen, to be rather handsome.

Bartemus Trollbane. A dwarf who is the ringmaster of a traveling circus and captain of the *Chainbreaker*. The Daughters Daring suspect he is also the notorious **Pirate Blacktoe**, but there is more to him than meets the eye.

Jolaia Serendi: A fierce and lovely Dublarian girl. Taken in as an orphan by Bartemus, Jolaia wishes only to free her people from the chains of slavery. As a master of blades, she becomes a mentor and friend to Emily Daring.

King Lamont: A wise and just king, but also weary. Lamont wishes to move his kingdom towards a more representative form of government but has underestimated the dangers that lie ahead. His history with the spider queen haunts him as well.

Annie Whipperpeel: Annie is everyone's favorite baker of delightful goods. But Annie has dark secrets of her own that involve more than just baking.

Jefferson & Gordon Black: Nefarious mercenaries, the Brothers Black hire out their combination of sword and sorcery to the highest bidders. But what happens when Gordon, a fearsome half-orc, develops feelings for a human girl?

Randolph of the Forest Gnomes: The unofficial leader of the tinkering gnomes, Randolph is older and wise for his kind. He now serves as liaison to the Knights Council.

Iris of the Faeries: A childhood friend of Aryanna Daring. Iris unwittingly helps point

Elizabeth Daring in the direction of dangerous adventure.

Evelyn the Spider Witch: Newcynder's "new queen." With an army at her disposal, how long before she returns to attack Highcynder again?

Gharidians: Peaceful, amphibian creatures. Gharidians look much like a gavial that can walk on two feet and speak. They are prized as slaves by Newcynder, however, and forced to dive for crystals in dangerous waters.

Harpies: Ancient creatures. Said to have once been human witches, but now with wings, feathers, and deadly talons. The harpies keep to themselves atop Mount Cynder, but Elizabeth Daring would disturb them in her quest for power.

The Skeleton King. Believed to be a long-deceased necromancer, the skeleton king waits to suck the life from his victims and regain his power over the living world.

STEVEN J. THOMPSON

About the Author

Steven J. Thompson was born and raised in Northern California. He left home to serve in the United States Army and returned later to raise a family and complete his education. A father of three, Steven entertained his own daughters with bedtime stories of adventurous young girls who were not afraid to face the world. After years of service as an Army Reserve Drill Sergeant, he is now putting these stories in print with the Daughters Daring, a new series with more to come. These are stories that encourage children, especially young girls, to be brave and daring. He and his family hope you will enjoy them.

Made in the USA
Columbia, SC
17 December 2019